"I know something's bothering you, Kellan."

"I'm bothered that your baby's dad left you both like he did," he replied.

Paige's level gaze told him she didn't believe him. "I can tell something's off, and it's not just that. You've done this before with me—I say something that upsets you and you don't tell me. Please let me make it right. Let me help you."

She couldn't. No one could. He'd hurt Paige if he shared this burden. Unless he was hurting her more by not telling her the truth. She deserved to know how her brother died, didn't she?

Kellan was tempted to tell her. Tempted by the relief that honesty always brought, even when the truth stung. And oh, how this truth would inflict damage. And Paige would hate him. He'd lose her from his life forever…

Susanne Dietze began writing love stories in high school, casting her friends in the starring roles. Today she's blessed to be the author of over half a dozen historical romances. Married to a pastor, and mom of two, Susanne loves fancy-schmancy tea parties, cozy socks and curling up on the couch with a costume drama and a plate of nachos. You can find her online at www.susannedietze.com.

Books by Susanne Dietze

Love Inspired

Widow's Peak Creek
A Future for His Twins
Seeking Sanctuary

Love Inspired Historical

The Reluctant Guardian
A Mother for His Family

Visit the Author Profile page at Harlequin.com.

Seeking Sanctuary

Susanne Dietze

LOVE INSPIRED

INSPIRATIONAL ROMANCE

LOVE INSPIRED®
INSPIRATIONAL ROMANCE

Recycling programs
for this product may
not exist in your area.

ISBN-13: 978-1-335-55436-9

Seeking Sanctuary

Copyright © 2021 by Susanne Dietze

This edition published by arrangement with Harlequin Books S.A.

For questions and comments about the quality of this book,
please contact us at CustomerService@Harlequin.com.

Love Inspired
22 Adelaide St. West, 40th Floor
Toronto, Ontario M5H 4E3, Canada
www.Harlequin.com

Printed in U.S.A.

Bear ye one another's burdens,
and so fulfill the law of Christ.
—*Galatians* 6:2

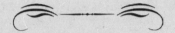

To Laura Hopkins.
Thanks for making me laugh and being there
for me since I was eleven. And to the
bossy girl who shoved us together as seventh
grade science partners, without whom I might
never have become best friends with my La.

Chapter One

For the first time since she learned to read as a seven-year-old, Paige Faraday entered a bookstore with no intention of buying anything. She might be a huge reader, but she hadn't driven over two hours from San Jose to the Sierra Nevada foothills because she wanted to pick up another paperback.

She'd come because she needed to find a man.

To *talk* to a particular man. If she could only locate him among the Saturday afternoon shoppers, that is.

Smoothing her denim jacket over her daffodil-yellow dress, Paige studied the checkout counter. Nope, he wasn't there, ringing up customers. Nor was he down the first few aisles, assisting patrons.

He had to be around here somewhere, though. He was the boss here at Open Book.

It was a special bookstore, drawing Paige to drop in whenever she visited her great-aunt here in Widow's Peak Creek. Perhaps it was the character of the shop, with its historic construction, cream-and-green exterior facade, exposed brick interior walls and charmingly creaky wood floors.

Maybe it was the leather-and-paper smell of the place, or the way Dr. Seuss quotes had been stenciled on the stairs to the children's section on the second floor. Whatever the reason, whenever Paige visited Open Book, she wanted to read anything and everything in the store.

Not just *wanted*. *Needed*, like she was greedy for words and knowledge.

She might not be able to afford another book anytime soon, though, if she didn't find Kellan Lambert.

Her gaze shifted toward the reading nook at the back of the store, a cozy space near the staircase set up with comfy leather chairs. A blond man in a blue Oxford shirt tucked into khaki chinos shook out a black tablecloth and then spread it over a rectangular folding table. His back was to her so she couldn't see his face, but with that lean cyclist's build and tall frame, who else could it be?

Now that she'd found him, her heart started pounding. So hard she couldn't move, much less breathe. *Lord, why am I stuck all of a sudden?* This was not the time to turn chicken.

As if in answer to her prayer, her legs twitched. *Let's do this.* She marched up behind the man at the table.

"Kellan Lambert?"

He spun around, brows risen in expectation.

Before either could say a word, a slip of a young woman with bubblegum-pink hair dashed into the reading nook. "Kellan?" Her voice rang with panic.

Since the woman was clearly an employee, with an Open Book name tag pinned to her black shirt, Paige deferred to Pink Hair with a wave. "Go ahead, please."

Kellan acknowledged Pink Hair with a brief nod before returning his gaze to Paige. "It's all right. Customers are always our top priority." So much for his recognizing her on sight. Since it had been a long time since their last in-person meeting, though, she hadn't expected him to. Her hair was longer now, not to mention she'd put on a few pounds. "How may I help you?"

His lips stretched into a courteous smile.

Courteous…and way too attractive. It was the sort of smile that could weaken a gal's knees, if she wasn't braced for impact. She'd noticed that smile before, of course. At their first meeting, she'd determined Kellan to be as handsome as he was nice, with his mussed curly hair and bright blue eyes.

But he'd been friends with her brother, Drew, which had rendered Kellan off-limits from the get-go. Regardless, she had *not* come to Widow's Peak Creek for romance.

Quite the opposite. She was here to focus on herself.

Well, herself and Peanut. Everything was about her unborn baby now.

She could wait five more minutes, though, so she met Kellan's tempting smile. "It's okay, honest. I'm not here as a customer."

His eyes widened. "Ah, I know just who you are, then."

"Oh, that's great." He recognized her, after all. That made things easier.

"I've been waiting for you." He thumped a palm on one of the cardboard boxes. "I was just about to unpack these for the signing, but since you're here, I don't want to mess up your system. I'll come back and check on you in a minute, okay?"

At once, her eye caught on the vertical vinyl

banner beside the table. It depicted a book cover—suspense, judging by the graphic of a broken mirror on it—and a headshot of a bearded guy named Norman Nickelby, author.

Oh, dear. Kellan thought she worked for the author.

It wasn't worth correcting him now, not when he was so busy. Whoever he'd expected to show up and unpack boxes was late, and Pink Hair was still waiting, a fretful crease between her heavily plucked eyebrows.

Paige had nothing better to do while she waited for him, anyway, so she nodded. "Sure thing, Kellan."

"Thanks a million." He strode quickly to the checkout counter with Pink Hair. "What's up, Mickcy? The credit card reader again?"

Paige grimaced. A faulty card reader would be a huge problem for a retail business, especially on a day with a special event like a book signing. Kellan had already opened the boxes, so she opened the flaps. The intoxicating odor of fresh paperbacks swirled around her as she pulled out a copy to peruse the back cover blurb. Spies and secrets. Sounded fun.

So how should she do this? It seemed reasonable to stack the books in a neat, inviting fashion, spine facing out, leaving a space in the middle of the table for the author to engage with readers. Right? She set to work, making adjustments here and there.

Hopefully, Kellan wouldn't mind how it looked. He'd always struck her as an easygoing guy, as flexible as he was kind. He was the sort of man who'd once told her she could come to him if she ever needed anything, and he'd meant it.

Which was why she was here.

A flutter of nerves prickled her stomach. Talking to him wasn't going to be easy, but it had to be done. "There's a blue sky behind those dark clouds," she murmured. Her motto. A reminder that the sun still shone brightly, even if she couldn't see it through her troubles.

She was almost finished stacking the books when Kellan returned, his rolled-up shirtsleeves revealing the corded muscles of his forearms. "Looks terrific, but I guess you're used to doing this sort of thing."

"I've never done this before in my life."

"Really? Could've fooled me." Kellan rubbed the faint blond stubble on his chin. "Hey, I forgot you requested the use of two acrylic J-stands to display books. Be right back."

Oh, dear, he needed to know she wasn't who he thought she was. And she had no idea what an acrylic J-thingie was. "But—"

He disappeared through a door beneath the staircase marked Employees Only that led to what appeared to be a hallway. Paige's spirits deflated. This might not have been the best time to drop in, unannounced, on Kellan. He was trying to earn a living and she was interrupting just to ask him for a favor.

In the meantime, she might as well finish up here, so she tucked the empty boxes beneath the table, hidden behind the black polyester tablecloth. She centered the author's chair, noticing yet another box on the seat. This one was full of bookmarks emblazoned with the book cover, a crystal bowl and a bag of Hershey's Kisses.

Whoever was supposed to be doing this might not like her taking over, but maybe they'd be grateful, so she fanned out the bookmarks. Helping people was easy. Receiving help? Not so much. Maybe that was why she'd hesitated earlier before approaching Kellan. Asking for help made her cringe inside, but this wasn't about her. It was all about Peanut, so she'd swallowed her pride and come.

Paige dumped wrapped Hershey's Kisses into the bowl—little gifts for the readers, she guessed—and prayed, asking for words to say to Kellan. How to start this conversation?

Kellan, it's been a while, no see. Do you remember me yet?

Kellan, hi, I'm Drew Faraday's sister.

Kellan? I'm Paige Faraday, and more than anything else in the world right now, I need your help.

More of a walk-in closet, the storeroom wasn't large enough to hold a lot of extra stock, but Kellan didn't mind. He'd traded space for character when he decided to run an independent bookstore out of a hundred-and-seventy-year-old building. But it also meant he had to be creative when storing things in this cramped space, so he had to dig under a package of paper coffee cups for the box he needed. Ah, there it was, with "signings" marked in Sharpie on the side.

He dug through the box, almost grateful for the chance to catch his breath.

He'd been running all day, since one of the dogs woke him up over an hour early. Good thing, too, because one of the sprinklers in the backyard had busted, shooting a fountain of water twelve feet high. He fixed it, but it had cost him precious time on an already busy day.

Help, Lord. Kellan had been praying the same two words for over five minutes already.

Any minute now, the featured author would

be here for the book signing. Norman wasn't local, but he was a hiker, and he often stopped into Open Book on his way to hike at higher elevations in the nearby Sierra Nevada Mountains. As far as Kellan was concerned, the signing would be a success if it blessed Norman as well as readers.

Kellan's silent partner, however, wanted the signing to bless the store. Through a large volume of sales.

Kellan and his partner, Don Phelps, had shared a similar vision of the store when they opened Open Book nearly four years ago, but their perspectives diverged lately. Sure, it would be nice for Open Book to see a bump in sales from the event, but Kellan wasn't as fixated on profits as Don, who was becoming less and less silent in his role as silent partner.

And it had become harder to discuss their differences since Don married Kellan's mom last year, making them family.

Sort of.

Family implied a sense of understanding, and no matter how much Kellan's mom, Don, or his sister in New York cared about him, they didn't get him. Not when it came to his relationship with God, and not in regard to how he'd changed since his return from Afghanistan. He wasn't the same person anymore.

How could he be, after what happened there? He should be dead. If it hadn't been for Drew Faraday—

Kellan shoved that last thought away. Reflecting on the loss of his best friend in the army was not something he could do at work. Not if he was going to get through this author signing.

He found the acrylic display stands and re-entered the store. The woman in the jean jacket fussed with the bookmarks on the table. A section of her long brown hair fell over her shoulder, obscuring her face, but something about her seemed familiar. She must've been in the store before. "Thanks for waiting. I have the display stands."

She reached for them and set one on each end of the table, angled for better viewing from the customers' side. "Please change this if it isn't right. I have no idea what bookstores, or authors, want in situations like these."

"But aren't you—don't you work for Norman?"

She shook her head. "Never met the man. Sorry, I just thought I'd pitch in. You seemed so busy."

Not that her help wasn't appreciated, but the last thing he needed was to violate some sort of labor law by putting a nonemployee to work.

"I thought you were Norman's assistant. She should've been here by now. I am so sorry."

"I didn't mind, Kellan. It was funny."

Oh, yeah, she'd known his name. Now that he had a spare second to look at her, recollection flooded him. How could he have forgotten those dark eyes and that impish smile, even for a moment? With her yellow dress poking out beneath the denim jacket, she looked like sunshine in a blue sky, familiar and sweet.

"I'm Paige Faraday," she said before he could speak the name on his tongue. "Drew's sister."

"Of course. I'm sorry I didn't recognize you right away." Their handshake was less of a formal greeting and more the lingering clasp of people who hadn't seen one another in a while, unsure if it was okay to hug.

"I totally understand." She waved her free hand. "You're really busy right now."

Life could get busy, but Kellan decided long ago that no one should ever feel unwelcome in his store, or in his life. Kellan saw it as a way to share Jesus with those around him. But when it came to Paige Faraday, Kellan gave himself a swift mental kick for not recognizing her immediately. She was important. Special. He'd roll up his sleeve right this minute if Drew's sister needed blood.

"There's never a bad time, Paige."

"I like that about you, Kellan. You're so good at putting people at ease."

She liked something about him? Why did that make his mouth go dry? "What's up?"

"I hoped we could chat for a minute, but my timing isn't great, is it?" She reached for a copy of Norman's book. As she stretched, her free hand went to the side of her stomach, like it was bracing.

Not bracing. Cupping. A bump.

All the blood in his head drained to his feet.

Her lips twitched as she noted his hasty attempt to look away. "I'm expecting, yeah."

He thought his mouth was dry a second ago? Now he could barely speak. "I am so sorry I put you to work like that. Lifting books. Are you okay?"

"The books weigh, like, nothing, and I've been sitting in a car for so long, it felt good to stand for a while. I'm fine, honest, or I wouldn't have done it."

He still felt awful. "You're sure?"

"I'm honestly happy to have helped a tiny bit, busy as you are. I feel bad monopolizing you now, but after the signing, do you have a few minutes?" Her smile faded. "I hate to even do this, but at Drew's funeral, you said if I ever needed help, I could come to you."

"I did."

And he would, right now. Norman wasn't here yet, so he had time. "What's going on, Paige? Is it your aunt? It is an aunt, right?" Paige's relative lived at Creekside Retirement Village, same as Gran.

"My great-aunt Trudie's just fine, thanks, and she's part of why I've come to Widow's Peak Creek. I need a short-term place to clear my head and figure a few things out for me and the baby." As she patted her stomach with a ringless hand, Kellan realized she hadn't mentioned the baby's father. Wasn't he in the picture? "Anyway," she continued, "I'll ask my question and get out of your hair. Do you know of anyone hiring temporary workers around here? Anyone who's desperate enough to take me on, that is?"

Her sunbeam of a smile lightened her last words. And broke his heart a little bit, too. That was all she wanted of him? A direction in which to pound the pavement?

"What type of work do you do, Paige? You're a server in a restaurant, right?"

"I was, yes, but for over a year now I've worked toward becoming a preschool teacher." She pulled a face. "I *was working* on it, I mean. And will again, but for now any sort of job would do, as long as it pays enough for me to eat on."

"Then you've got a job here, if you want it."

Her eyes widened. "You have an opening?"

"Yep." As of two seconds ago. Kellan usually prayed about things like hiring, and he should've looked at the books, especially since Don was already breathing down his neck about trimming expenses so they could expand to a second store.

But Paige was Drew Faraday's little sister—his pregnant little sister—and Drew was the reason Kellan still drew breath. Clearly, she needed a haven from whatever storm had brought her here.

He understood that need all too well. That was why he'd settled here four years ago, in the town where Gran and Pop retired. There was something about the fresh air, mountain views and history of this California gold rush-era community that seemed to offer sanctuary to a troubled mind.

"Welcome to Widow's Peak Creek and Open Book, for however long or short you need." He thrust out his hand, one person seeking peace to another.

Chapter Two

Paige clasped both hands around Kellan's warm one. A job in this bookstore? With a guy like Kellan for a boss?

Yes, please.

What were the chances he needed help right when she needed a job? No, not chance. God's intervention. That was what it was.

Paige had a million questions, but she'd cornered Kellan long enough. She let go of his hand. "Is there a good time to discuss the details?"

"I'm flexible." Kellan glanced at his smart watch. "Where are you staying?"

Aside from finding a job, that was the other area where she was looking for God's quick provision. Hopefully, an affordable Airbnb. "I'm not sure yet."

"If you don't have anything lined up yet, I've

got the perfect place. Well, Marigold and I do. Little guesthouse we use for family visits and vacation rentals. We're vacant for the foreseeable future, though, thanks to a busted kitchen pipe. I removed the listing while I repaired it, so it's yours as long as you're in town."

First of all, who was Marigold? His wife? He wasn't wearing a wedding ring, but boy, was it a good thing she'd stopped herself from fixating on Kellan's delightful smile.

Second, as long as she was in town? No way. She had no idea how long that would be, and while she'd saved enough to live on until after Peanut was born, she couldn't say yes sight unseen to a place that might not be a good fit for her budget.

Third, and most important, she hadn't intended for Kellan to help her beyond sharing a few suggestions of where to look for work. She must not rely on him, or anyone, ever again. Not even a little bit. She should, as her mom always said, stand on her own two feet.

But right then those two feet let her know in no uncertain terms they were finished with the day. Her ankles joined the chorus, throbbing out an SOS—*elevate us, please.*

Swollen ankles were a new experience for Paige, but she'd read they weren't uncommon in pregnancy. Nor was her sudden hunger.

Truth be told, it would be nice to pick up a few groceries and prop up her feet…the sooner the better.

One night, then. Tomorrow she could hunt for a new place to live, but tonight she'd stay at Kellan and Marigold's. Whoever Marigold was.

She was about to ask the nightly rental rate when Kellan's attention diverted to a gray-headed man entering the store. She'd seen a lot of the man's face in the past several minutes, stacking his books, so she held up her hands. "Your author's here. We can talk later."

"Thanks for understanding. I'm sorry I don't have the key on me, but could you meet me there in, say, three hours? Sorry that's such a long time, but I'm stuck right now."

"Three hours gives me time to grab groceries. Thanks, Kellan." She typed his address into her phone.

Out in the midafternoon sunshine, she strolled to her baby blue Volkswagen bug. Settling into the driver's seat, she cracked the windows, kicked off her flats and wiggled her toes. *Thanks, God.* Did He mind if she prayed while she ate the protein bar she'd tucked in her purse? She hadn't been a churchgoer for long, but she'd been told she could talk to God anytime, so surely He didn't mind a pregnant woman's conversation while she snacked.

Thanks for a job and somewhere to sleep tonight. Show me how to make it up to Kellan.

She had to pay him back somehow. She wouldn't be a charity case. Just thinking about it made her stomach cramp around her protein bar. If her mother could see her right now, she'd—

Enough of that line of thinking. She shut her eyes, trying to shove away the bad thoughts and replace them with good things. Things that would lower her blood pressure. Things like God's love. Poppies waving in the breeze. The smell of paperback books, fresh from the box. Pickles, crisp and tart.

Her eyes flew open and her hand went to her demanding stomach. She needed a pickle. Right now. She started the engine. Good thing she had some time to kill.

Kellan hated being late.

Normally his punctuality, or lack of it, wasn't a huge issue, but he'd told Paige he'd meet her at the house fifteen minutes ago…and she'd already waited three hours before that. His stomach clenched as he pulled his crew cab truck out of the parking lot behind Open Book to turn onto Main Street. Or tried to, anyway. Traffic was thick. Little wonder, with this being close to dinnertime on a Saturday in early summer, and Main Street was a tourist trap of shops and restaurants, all wood and brick buildings original to the town's founding in the 1850s.

Much as he usually loved the slower pace of this small town, though, he was in a massive hurry. Four years ago he'd offered to help Paige if she ever needed it. And now that she needed it, he was failing at the opportunity. He was failing Drew.

In an instant, Kellan's brain flashed back to Afghanistan and the night of Drew's death. How it was all Kellan's fault. Only a few people outside the Army knew the truth, how Kellan had directed his squad to take a particular route, based on advice from a trusted ally. An man who, it turned out, wasn't an ally, after all. He'd sent them into a trap, and Kellan was supposed to have been the one to die. He would have, too, if Drew hadn't switched places with him at the last second—

Kellan shoved his thoughts away. Now was not the time to let those memories take center stage in his brain. He had to get to Paige, who, along with her mom, Joyce, didn't know the whole story about Drew's death. It was supposed to stay that way, too. His superior officers had said Drew's family deserved peace after "the incident," as they called it. They'd told Paige and Joyce that Drew had been killed by insurgents during an ambush, but no more than that. Kellan was told to keep his mouth shut about the tragedy and move on.

He'd kept his mouth shut, but moving on? Impossible.

Every day, he woke up bearing the burden of Drew's death. But he also awoke knowing God allowed him to live for a reason. He'd determined to help others to repay God for His gift of life. In Drew's last moments, Kellan promised his friend he'd do whatever he could for Joyce and Paige.

Here was a small opportunity to do that, but he was stuck, rapping his thumbs against the steering wheel, wanting to tear out into the middle of traffic.

Kellan took a deep breath. Time to remember God was in charge and trust Him with all of this. He felt his shoulders relax at the realization.

Within minutes he turned into his neighborhood, making the final turn onto a shade-lined street full of craftsman-style houses. A baby blue Volkswagen Bug was parked in front of his house, directly beneath the American sweetgum tree. Was it Paige's?

Her shaded silhouette was still in the driver's seat, so once he parked he jogged to her car, unsure what to expect. She had every right to be annoyed, tired and armed with a disappointed sigh for him. But he hadn't expected her to be asleep behind the steering wheel, paperback on her lap, a dewy jar of refrigerated pickles on the passenger seat.

She looked…sweet. No other word for it, her soft lips parted, her dark lashes fanning her cheeks. Surely, she needed rest. But not like this. He wouldn't leave his dogs locked in a car, even with the windows cracked, on a temperate day.

He curled his fingers and rapped on the window.

Paige rubbed her eyes. And then jumped out of her skin at the sight of the man looming at her through the window, blond brows knit.

Kellan's brows shifted to convey apology. "Sorry to wake you."

Blinking, she opened the car door. "I didn't plan to drift off." But she must have, since her last thoughts of eating a sandwich had to have been a dream. If she was trying to make an impression as a bright-eyed and bushy-tailed employee, she'd utterly failed.

"No, it's my fault. I took longer than I said I would."

She glanced at the clock on the dashboard. "Twenty minutes is not that long, Kellan. I haven't been here long, anyway."

She'd driven up to the house and sighed with envy at the dove-gray dwelling, trimmed in white. Tapered white columns supported the roof over the deep front porch, where white Adirondack chairs offered a place to sit and enjoy the landscaping of drought-tolerant plants edging a grassy lawn. She'd thought about sitting up there, but instead, she'd decided to stay in the car, shaded by the sweet-gum tree that would be majestic come autumn.

And apparently fallen asleep, but she was wide-awake now. Embarrassment was clearly a more efficient way to get moving than coffee. She hopped out of her car. "This is gorgeous, Kellan."

"Thanks. It's been fun to spruce up the place. Anyway, come on in so I can get the key."

"You did this? And fixed a pipe, you said. If you ever decide to get out of bookselling, you could have a career as a contractor." She followed him up the porch steps.

The moment his key hit the lock, a chorus of woofs carried through the door. He had dogs.

A dozen, by the sound of it. "How many are in there?"

"Just two, but they're on the big side."

How big? Paige braced herself as he opened the door. Then she let out a squeal of delight as she met the soulful stares of two dogs, one fluffy and white, the other speckled brown and three-legged.

"Look at your guys." Her voice went up two octaves.

"The white one's Gladys, and the spotted one's Jet."

"Hi, babies." As Paige rubbed them both down, their thick tails wagged, whapping against her legs. After a few moments they looked up at Kellan.

"Yeah, yeah," he said in a teasing voice. "I'm chopped liver compared to new people. Come on in, Paige. Maybe Frank will greet you, too."

"Is Frank a roommate?" What about Marigold?

"Frank's a cat."

The dogs followed after her into a minimally decorated living room that lacked framed photos or knickknacks of any kind. A plush gray rug softened the room, as did two large dog cushions by the fireplace hearth and a tasteful abstract painting in shades of gray. The only signs of clutter were a stocked bookcase and a pile of remotes mounded atop the coffee table in front of a large-screen TV. If Marigold was his wife, she'd let Kellan do the decorating.

"So who's Marigold?"

"My neighbor." He said it with such affection, Paige wondered if *neighbor* also meant *girlfriend*. It wouldn't surprise her that Kellan was taken. Marigold was probably drop-dead gorgeous and as sweet as peach pie, too.

Following him into the kitchen, she could see out the back windows that the driveway beside his house went all the way back behind his house and his neighbor's. Marigold's, apparently. "She won't mind that I'm here?"

"I texted her already, and she's delighted." He handed her the key. "Come on, I'll show you the house."

He took her out to the backyard through a patio door, Gladys and Jet racing past them. Then he pointed through a chain-link fence at the sweetest little cottage she'd ever seen. "There it is."

"A tiny house?"

"Hope it suits you." He led her through the chain-link gate, nudging Jet and Gladys back into the yard as they went.

Two-storied, long and wide as an RV, the tiny house had been given a craftsman-style look, but it was white with black trim. Kellan, or the mysterious Marigold, had planted annuals in a black wood box beside the small porch, including Iceland poppies, her favorite. Swaying on their long stems, the petals' hues reminded her of fruit sherbets, orange, lemon, strawberry.

"Kellan, it's wonderful."

"Head on in, and I'll get your stuff."

"You don't need to do that."

"I want to. May I have your keys?"

She should do it herself, but his expression brooked no argument. She handed over her key ring and let herself into the tiny house, gasping in delight. The place smelled like lemongrass, and everything was decorated in neutral shades with pops of teal and tangerine. Kellan had definitely not done the decorating.

She walked through the sitting area, complete with a love seat and narrow recliner opposite a small television mounted on the wall and a tiny table with two folding chairs. Beyond the tight spiral staircase to the loft above—the bedroom, no doubt—lay a compact kitchen with a two-burner stove, a minuscule oven no self-respecting Thanksgiving turkey could get a wing into and a mini fridge. Just behind that was a three-quarters bathroom, compact but functional.

It was perfect, all of it.

"Coming in," Kellan announced before he carried in her tote, hanging bag, food cooler, rolling suitcase and an aluminum tray that was definitely not hers, all balanced like the convoluted pieces in a game of Tetris. He lowered everything but the suitcase onto the love seat. "I'll haul this one upstairs for you. Don't want you falling off balance."

Before she'd unpacked the cooler, he'd bounded back downstairs and scooped up the aluminum tray. "I brought you dinner."

So that was what that was? "Seriously? You shouldn't have."

"Frozen lasagna. It's close to dinnertime so you can eat it tonight, but you can save it for a rainy day if you'd rather."

She'd accepted more help from him today than she had from anyone since childhood, maybe. A job, shelter, carrying her bags and now lasagna? It was too much, and if she didn't do something to even the score between them, even a little, she'd do something stupid and embarrassing and burst into tears.

"Tonight would be great. You and Marigold have to eat it with me, though. I picked up salad fixings that will go with it."

"Marigold's at her granddaughter's tonight, but I'm in."

Granddaughter? Marigold was definitely not

on Kellan's dating radar, then. For some dumb reason, Paige felt relieved at the news.

How silly.

He moved to the door, hand on the knob. "I've got some things to see to before dinner. Need anything else right now, or shall I see you in an hour?"

"An hour's great." She'd have cash out to pay him for the night's rent. But first things first. This lasagna needed to get into the oven if they were going to eat it in an hour. He opened the door but paused in the threshold. "Tell your mom hi for me, when you let her know you're settling in."

"What?" She looked up.

"Parents worry about stuff like that. I know how it is."

No, he didn't. He didn't at all.

Paige's arms went cold, and it had nothing to do with the frozen lasagna clutched in both hands.

Chapter Three

The gold light of evening was fading when Kellan swallowed his last bite of the lasagna, as delicious as his first, with the creamy ricotta a perfect complement to the basil-infused meat sauce. "Want another helping, Paige?"

Her hands rested over her stomach. "I'm stuffed. This was delicious, better than any frozen lasagna I've ever had."

"Emerald's, the restaurant next door to Open Book, has frozen casserole specials every week. I like to keep a few on hand for times like these."

"Like when your old army buddy's sister drops in unexpectedly?" Her teasing grin revealed a becoming dimple in each cheek.

"Pretty much." He liked that she felt at ease teasing him, and it was easy to tease her back.

"So how's your mom doing? She must be excited about having a grandbaby."

He'd thought it would be a pleasant topic of conversation, but her dimples disappeared. "I said the wrong thing."

"No, it's just that she, um, doesn't know about the baby yet."

Kellan took a sip of water, less out of thirst and more to buy him time before he spoke. Why hadn't she shared such important news with Joyce?

None of his business. Just Paige's and the baby's father's, whoever he was. Wherever he was. He didn't want to pry, but it might be helpful to know a few details before he said the wrong thing. Again. "Does your mom know you're in Widow's Peak Creek?"

Her features softened. "Yes. I texted her this morning before I left, informing her Aidan and I broke up. My classes are finished for the semester, so there's nothing keeping me in San Jose. And she knows I've always had a soft spot for Widow's Peak Creek, so she wasn't surprised I chose to come here for a while." She stared at her empty plate. "It's probably wrong, not telling her about Peanut, but I can't. Not yet."

A hundred questions formed on Kellan's

tongue, but the first one out of his mouth was, "Peanut?"

"The baby. That's been the nickname for a while now, even though he or she is a lot bigger than a peanut now. I'm five months along, so maybe it's more like a cantaloupe."

Cantaloupe-sized was still pretty small for a human being. Fingers, toes and a beating heart. It was incredible, amazing and at the same time sad that she was going through this by herself.

"I'm sorry about the breakup." As well as whatever was keeping her from telling her mom. "That sounds rough."

"Thanks. It's been hard, for sure." Paige scraped excess lasagna from the serving spoon onto her plate. "I met Aidan, Peanut's dad, at a wedding last autumn. He lived in San Jose, I lived in Sacramento, not too far apart but not close, either."

"Not the easiest on a relationship."

"We were fine with the long distance thing, so I was shocked when he called to gush over a rental house he'd found, but he was stuck in the lease on his apartment for another six months. A house that nice wouldn't sit empty for long, so he suggested I live in it. That meant switching colleges and quitting my job at the preschool where I was earning observation hours.

Naturally, I balked. I wasn't going to leave my life behind so I could housesit for him. But then he proposed to me..."

Her voice trailed off. Kellan waited for her to finish, his gut aching for her.

"I wanted to start a life. A family. So I went. But, as is now obvious, things didn't work out. It all went south when I found out I was pregnant." She made a noise like a whistle of wind.

"He left?"

"He didn't go anywhere, exactly. You're familiar with the term *ghosting*?"

"Are you serious? He ignored you?"

"I left messages on his phone. I emailed him. I drove to his apartment." She ticked the items off on her fingers. "I checked in at his work to make sure he wasn't in the hospital or something, but no, he was working. Just 'too busy right now.' So I left a message saying I would wait until he was ready to discuss things. Fast-forward to two days ago, when he let me know things were over for good, in regard to both me and the baby."

Kellan's fists clenched on his lap. What kind of man was this coward, abandoning his unborn child and pregnant fiancée like that? People did stupid things when they got scared, sure, but this didn't sound like the frantic act of a frightened kid. It sounded calculated. Cold.

Kellan would have given anything for a family, for a pretty fiancée whose smile was like sunshine—

Whoa. He knew better than to go down that road. He was not family material.

That didn't mean he was made of stone, though. If Afghanistan hadn't happened, Kellan would have fought hard to protect what this idiot Aidan gave away.

But Afghanistan *had* happened, and Kellan was forever in Drew Faraday's debt. He would do everything he could to help Drew's little sister. He should say something soothing.

"That guy's a jerk," he said instead.

"I'm not a fan of how he handled it, either," Paige continued as if she were reading a story that happened to someone else. Probably because it hurt less that way. "But it wasn't all bad. That whole time I was waiting for him to figure things out, I started going to church." Her face softened. "It's given me peace, which I really need right now. If it wasn't for God, I don't know what I would have done when Aidan formalized things."

The word sounded strange. "What do you mean, *formalized*?"

"A courier delivered two things to me. A legal document where he relinquishes all rights to the baby, and an eviction notice from the landlord."

Kellan's head went hot. Hot enough to turn his vision red. "He kicked you out of the house?"

"It turns out my name was never on the lease. I'd signed an agreement, but it wound up being fake. Can you imagine what sort of person gives his fiancée a sham lease to sign?" She laughed, a complete one-eighty from Kellan's emotional state.

"Paige, that's awful."

"You're not wrong." She rose and carried their plates to the tiny sink. "So I'm officially homeless, jobless, expecting a baby and unsure what to do about my remaining college courses. The only thing I know for sure is that I am never getting involved with a man again, because no way is Peanut ever attaching to someone who's going to hurt him or her. But beyond that? I don't have a plan. Once I received those documents, the only thing I could think of was Widow's Creek Peak. How quiet and sweet it is here. It seemed like a good place to figure things out, so here I am."

"You're going to thrive here, too." Kellan's tone and words hid the rage boiling inside him. He wished he could punch something. Instead, he covered the lasagna pan with its foil lid and stuffed it into the mini fridge.

"I'm not the same person I was five months ago, because of Jesus." Her voice rose over the water as she rinsed the plates. "I have a motto—*there's a blue sky behind those dark clouds*—but now that He's in my life? I believe that blue sky is because of Him. He'll see me through tough times. My mom won't understand that, though. She avoids church."

"I have a few issues with my mom and stepdad, so I can relate somewhat." They didn't go to church, either, and Don and Mom both had agendas when it came to Kellan. Don wanted to open a second bookstore, and Mom wanted—never mind.

"That's right, we both have single moms." Paige ducked under the sink and pulled out a bottle of dish soap.

Kellan's dad passed when he was in high school, which had been rough. But her dad? "I remember Drew saying he left when you were small."

"Totally out of the picture before I was two. Drew was four." She squirted the dish soap into the sink, filling the air with a lemony scent. "My mom had to learn how to handle everything from finances to home maintenance, fast. She didn't want us to be flat-footed like she was, so she made it clear to me and Drew we'd be on our own at eighteen. More than anything else in life, she wanted us to be completely independent. Capable. Certain. Which is why I'm not going to tell her about Peanut until I have a plan that proves I'm all those things."

"You already seem all of those things to me." Kellan tugged a clean dish towel from its peg by the oven and reached for the glass she rinsed.

"I've got you fooled, then," she said in her teasing voice, grinning.

It didn't take a genius to figure out she used humor as a diversion. She deflected pain with a smile or a joke, but it sure sounded like her mom's approval had been tied to Paige's ability to support herself in every way. While Kellan would argue that Paige was doing what she needed to do, that didn't mean she couldn't use some emotional support.

"The Bible wouldn't talk about bearing one another's burdens if we all didn't need help now and again, though. So know that I'm here for you. You're not asking. I'm offering."

"You've done more than enough, Kellan. A roof over my head tonight, a meal and a job, which by the way, we have to discuss." She scrubbed the plates now that they were finished with the glasses. "What time do you want me on Monday?"

He replayed her words back in his head as he put the dried glasses back in the cupboard. "*Tonight?* You're staying here as long as you're in town, aren't you?"

She bit her lip. "Actually, no. I'm going to look for a new place tomorrow."

Why? She didn't like it here? He was fond of the tiny house, but then again, he was invested in it. He looked around in an attempt to view through different eyes. "Yeah, it is pretty small."

"No, that's not it."

What else could it be? He followed her gaze out the window over the sink and realized what she'd been looking at. His house. From this angle, she had a view of the dogs frolicking in his backyard and could see straight through some of the windows into his house, too. His cat, Frank, perched on the windowsill of Kellan's home office as if it was his job to supervise the dogs.

Then it hit him.

"Are you concerned about propriety? That I live too close? Because Marigold keeps the spare key and keeps a clear eye on things, so if you're worried about me—"

"I'm not worried about you. Or this place.

I just don't want to impose on you any more than I already have."

"It's not an imposition. In fact, you're doing us a favor, if you stay."

"I doubt that. It's summer. You probably have regular clients who come every year for vacation, and pay top dollar for the experience, which, frankly, might be a little over my budget. Which reminds me, what's the nightly fee?"

He hadn't planned on charging her anything, actually, knowing Marigold wouldn't mind.

But Paige had talked about her family valuing complete independence. He knew in his bones it would be a mistake to offer for her to stay for free, or even at a discount, no matter how great a debt he owed her brother, so he quoted her the rate per month.

Her brow arched with clear suspicion. "That's far too low for a vacation rental."

"The nightly rate is higher, yes, but Marigold and I tiered our pricing. The longer you stay the cheaper it is, because it's easier for us that way. Not that anyone's stayed for a month, but we offer that option." He could tell she still didn't believe him. "You can look it up online."

She stared at him before rolling her eyes. "All right, then."

"You'll stay?"

"I'll stay."

He couldn't help but smile back at her. She had that way about her, lightening the atmosphere even in the middle of a heavy discussion. But he had one last serious thing to say. "I sincerely hope you can rest and regroup while you're here, Paige. You need a break."

Her gasp wasn't quite the response he expected, but then her wide-eyed gaze met his. "The baby is moving. It feels—wow."

What did *wow* mean? Wow *nice* or wow, *danger was nigh*? "Do you need to sit down?"

"Oh, no, we're dancing in there." She burst into laughter.

He couldn't share in whatever she was experiencing, but he reveled in her happiness. Right then, he decided to do all he could to lighten her burdens, not add to them, during this tough time.

For four years he'd grappled with the secret he'd been keeping from Paige and her mom. He wanted to tell them what happened the night Drew died, but the warnings from his superiors rolled through his head again and again.

Keep it to yourself. You'll be glad you did.

Glad wasn't an accurate way to describe Kellan's feelings, even four years later. *Tortured*, more like. He could have ended that torture and told Paige the truth tonight.

But he wasn't going to dissolve the deep-dimpled smile of hers and add to her burdens. Not while she was figuring out a plan.

Maybe God agreed with Kellan's superiors in the army. The truth of Drew's death was better left buried in the desert sand.

That night Paige snuggled into the queen-size bed in the loft with a book, sinking against the mountain of soft pillows. Her swollen ankles, resting atop a small cushion, would have sighed with pleasure if they could've. *I'm so comfortable, God.* She'd formed the habit of talking to Him about the minuscule details of her life as well as the big ones. Hopefully, He didn't mind. She hadn't been going to church long enough to ask anyone such a question, and she hadn't found the answer yet in her new Bible.

Maybe she could ask Kellan. He'd been a Christian for a while, hadn't he? Since the army. Right now she could hear him calling the dogs inside. It wasn't overloud. It was sweet, actually. It felt soothing.

So soothing that she must've fallen asleep and not awakened until the sun shone bright yellow through the loft window. She checked the time on her phone and yelped. That late?

She'd also missed a text from Kellan, inviting her to church. Almost two hours ago. He didn't list the time for services, but she'd probably missed it. Just in case, she threw on a simple dress, wolfed down overnight oats flavored with coconut and honey and went outside.

"You must be Paige." A tiny woman in a turquoise tracksuit and cropped white hair waved from where she tended the rosebushes next door. Her voice was as high and cheerful as a Christmas elf's.

"And you must be Marigold." Paige hurried to shake her hand. How had she anticipated Marigold would be? Sweet as a peach pie and drop-dead gorgeous? Well, she was indeed kind and quite pretty. "Back from your granddaughter's?"

"Oh, yes, last night, and I attended early church. How did you sleep in our little guest cottage?"

"So well I dozed through Kellan's invitation to church. Looks like I missed him."

"He left over half an hour ago, but it appears you needed the rest." She snipped a drooping blossom. "I know your aunt Trudie, you know. We're in a knitting circle the first Tuesday of the month. Eileen, Kellan's grandma, is in it, too."

What a small town this was. A small world, even, since neither she nor Kellan had grown up here, but both had relatives in this tiny town who knew each other—and he and her brother had been in the same squad in Afghanistan. On Saturday she'd marveled at the way God had intervened by opening up a job for her, and this seemed to be yet another example of His hand.

"I feel like I've known Kellan a long time, even though he's only lived next door for a few years." Marigold swiped her hand over her sweaty, wrinkled brow before donning her glove again. "He and I used to stand here and stare at the vacant piece of land on our property line, where the tiny house is now, and one day we decided it might be a fun project. I wouldn't have gone into something like that little house with just anyone, though, dear Paige."

Thirty seconds into their acquaintance, and already Paige was *dear*. From some people, the endearment might have felt presumptuous, but from Marigold? It felt like a warm hug. "I can tell he thinks you're pretty special, too."

"Piffle." Marigold brushed off the comment, but she pinked with pleasure.

"Your roses are beautiful, but I love the Iceland poppies there. My favorite flower." Paige glanced back at the blooms in front of the tiny house. "When they bob in the breeze on those long stems, it looks like they're waving hello."

"You know, you're right." Marigold tipped her head to the side. "Alas, they'll fade by midsummer. But I'll have new ones in the ground come autumn, and other than a brief rest during the winter, they'll give us a show for several months."

Paige wouldn't be here then to see next year's flowers, so she would have to be mindful to enjoy these now. "I should go back inside and look for an online church service." And while she wasn't ready to tell her mom about Peanut, she should shoot her another text. Mom would want to know Paige's temporary address as well as where she'd found employment. "Have a nice day, Marigold."

"You, too, dear Paige. May the Lord watch over you today."

No one had ever said anything like that to Paige before, except during dismissal time at church. The realization made her feel blessed by Marigold's words, but also sad, because she'd missed out on God most of her life. If she'd trusted God earlier, maybe she wouldn't have dated Aidan. She wouldn't be expecting a baby in four months.

Mulling over *what-ifs* wouldn't do any good, though. Better to focus on what she had, which was a lot. God, His hope and, through Kellan, a job and shelter while she figured out what to do next.

She was grateful for all of it, and someday, when she was settled in a new town, holding her baby in her arms, she'd look back on her short time in Widow's Peak Creek with gratitude for God giving her a soft place to land for a little while.

Chapter Four

Monday morning Paige twisted her hair into a topknot and stared into her closet, eyeing her choices for her first day of work at Open Book. Outside, the morning sky was already bright blue and cloudless, promising another warm day. She chose a flowy green dress that complemented her coloring and accommodated her changing figure.

Would it still fit in a few months? *Lord, remind me to add maternity clothes to my budget next month.* Once Kellan gave her a tour of Open Book later that morning, however, it was obvious she'd have to add a small book allowance to her budget, too. "The temptation to buy everything in this store is strong," she teased. She was only slightly exaggerating.

"Thankfully, there's the employee discount." Kellan tapped a shelf, meeting her smile. "Otherwise, I wouldn't bring home enough of a paycheck to feed the dogs."

Mickey, the pink haired staff member, laughed. "You're not that bad, Kellan, but we all love books. That's why we work here."

Not quite, in Paige's case, but she agreed with the sentiment. "There's nothing like a good book."

"Or a magazine." Mickey eyed an older gentleman sitting in the overstuffed chair in the magazine section. One gnarled hand balanced an open periodical and the other held a cup of the free coffee Kellan offered.

Kellan gestured at the man. "Paige, meet Herb, one of our regulars."

"Hi." Her greeting was acknowledged with a nod and a slurp before the man returned his attention to the magazine.

Kellan leaned closer to Paige to whisper, "Don't take it personally. Herb's a quiet guy and he loves his coffee."

"Oh, I never underestimate a person's need for caffeine in the morning. Before Peanut, I needed two cups to get going. Alas, no caffeine for me right now." She pulled a comically sad face, which made Kellan laugh, as she hoped it would. "So, boss, now that we've finished the tour, what task do you have for me this morning?"

"We're not quite done with the tour, though."
Kellan rubbed his hands together. "Front north
corner of the store."

He led her around a bookcase near the front
window and gestured at a glass case tucked
against the wall. Inside it was—what on earth?

"An anvil?" And other metal tools. How had
she missed that hulking thing when she'd been
in here on Saturday? Why was it in a bookstore?

Maybe her lack of observation had to do
with how much she'd wanted to find Kellan.
Or maybe that bookcase had hidden it from
her view. Regardless, the anvil was significant somehow.

Kellan tapped the edge of the glass case.
"I'm sure you know Widow's Peak Creek was
built during the gold rush. Lots of history, but
the town lacks a museum, so for now, each
shop on Main Street showcases artifacts from
when the building was new. This used to be
a blacksmith, hence the display in here of the
original anvil and smithy tools."

"What a great idea."

"And on this shelf behind you are plenty
of books on local history, mining, and California flora and fauna. Occasionally, tourists
want reading material to supplement their experiences."

At once her mind went to preschool curriculum. "Kids' books, too?"

"No, everything for kids is upstairs." He rubbed the back of his neck. "Why? Do you think I should move some down here?"

"I do. Otherwise, families who look at the display might not be aware of what's available to enrich their kids' education. You've got a *golden* opportunity to spark imaginations right here. *Pun intended.*"

Kellan groaned at the joke, but right then Paige decided some hot day, her future preschool classes would pan for "gold" glitter out of a kiddie pool.

His groan didn't mean he didn't like the idea, though, because then he nodded. "You've been here half an hour and already you're improving things. I'll stock some kids' books on history and the gold rush down here today."

"Ah, I do love to hear you talk about town history, Kellan." A slight woman a few years older than Paige approached them, tucking her bobbed, dark blond hair behind her ear.

Kellan grinned. "Faith Latham, meet Paige Faraday, new to Widow's Peak Creek. Paige, Faith runs the antiques store a few doors up, and she's the one in charge of the museum artifacts."

Ah, now her comment about history made sense. "So creative."

"I can't take credit for coming up with the idea. That was Tom. But it's been a blessing while we work toward a permanent museum. Anyway, welcome to town. If you need anything, let me know."

Paige wouldn't be staying long enough to need much. It wasn't worth the whole speech, though, and Faith was just being nice. "I appreciate it. I'll have to visit your store."

"Honey? If you give me your magazines, I'll get in line at the register." A dark-haired man with a few days' worth of stubble on his jaw rounded the bookshelf. "Oh, sorry. Didn't see you guys. Hey, Kellan."

At once Kellan gestured at the man. "Paige, this is Tomás Santos, Faith's fiancé."

Ah, the Tom she'd mentioned. He took the magazines from Faith, all of which were of the bridal variety. They must be in the thick of wedding plans. "Congratulations."

"Thanks," Tom said. "I don't know who's more excited, us or the kids. I have six-year-old twins."

Twins. Oh, boy. Double the blessing, but at the moment a single infant seemed overwhelming enough to handle on her own.

I'm not alone, though, am I, God? You're

here. The reminder soothed the nerves that flared at the thought of raising the baby alone. Hopefully, no one noticed her momentary panic. "Best wishes on your wedding planning."

"Thanks so much." Faith turned an adoring gaze up at her fiancé. He grinned down at her, his expression as besotted as hers.

Paige had to look away. Not that she begrudged the couple their happiness, of course. It was just that since she'd chosen against ever having a future relationship, this was the first time she'd given any thought to exactly what that meant. She would never be looked at like Faith was right now. She would never have what they had.

None of that is as important as Peanut. That's why I made the decision to stay single, and that's why I'm here, right? She had a future to figure out.

And if the prospect of a lifetime alone stung? She'd make peace with it eventually. She had to, because her future most definitely did not include a husband.

Employees' first days on the job were not always the smoothest, for them or Kellan as their supervisor, but Paige fit right in with the patrons and staff alike. He observed her refill

Herb's coffee, help Mickey cull mystery books for the clearance table and engage customers of all ages.

She seemed at home no matter the task, with an ever-present smile on her face. It was the sort of smile that always coaxed one from him in return. How could he not admire her attitude, especially in light of all she was going through?

Broken engagements were rough enough, even when amicable. But her fiancé hadn't just broken up with her. No, he'd abandoned her. Her and her baby. And evicted her, like she'd been the one who'd done something wrong.

That Aidan guy had basically used her as a placeholder on a house. He must be one slick, conniving creep to have deceived Paige like that.

It was enough to make his blood churn, but she was right when she'd said God had a way of working things out. There was sometimes a lot of waiting between the now and the then, which required patience. And trust.

He'd be praying for her, to find the plan and path God had for her. That she could teach preschool sooner rather than later, as was her dream. That she could be all God had for her to be.

But right now he'd better focus on closing

out the register, since it was time to go home for the day.

He must have been more focused than he realized, because he didn't see Paige until she approached the register. Her purse hung over her shoulder and her arms were laden with books. A dozen, maybe.

Had she discovered defective books? Sometimes they had a way of getting bent or worn when folks browsed through them. "What's up with those?"

She dropped them onto the counter. "Nothing. I want to buy them."

"Putting the employee discount to good use already?" He peeked at the titles, all large print. "Cozy mystery fan, eh?"

"Sure, but these aren't for me. Aunt Trudie is expecting me now, over at Creekside. I thought it would be nice to bring a gift she could share with other residents."

How thoughtful. "Would you mind if the store covers the tab?"

"You don't need to do that. These are all on clearance."

The price wasn't what nagged at Kellan, though. "I should've thought of doing this a long time ago. Open Book sponsors book drives, donations, stuff like that all the time, but I never thought of giving any to Creekside." Or his own grandmother, who lived there. "In fact, if it's all right, I'd like to go over with you. It's been a while since I visited Gran. I'll text her and see if she's available."

"All right. If you're sure I didn't push you into covering these."

"No way." Although even as he rang up the books, his stomach burned. With shame, for not having been to Creekside in a while and for not having thought of sending books over there. But he had his reasons, and even now, he braced himself for the visit.

Lord, help. It was all he could think to pray.

Paige had never visited her aunt at Creekside, but as she parked her VW Bug beside Kellan's truck in the retirement village lot, she gave it a thorough once-over. The complex of buildings looked both tidy and homey. The main building, a Georgian-style brick structure, welcomed guests and residents, and she and Kellan walked into the lobby together. It smelled fresh and clean, and large windows let in the late-afternoon light. A directory mapped out the way to different buildings—condominiums, resident rooms and a special care wing—while a separate map indicated the dining room and a lounge were in this building.

Paige tapped the word *lounge* on the sign.

"That's where Aunt Trudie is meeting me," she told Kellan, loud enough for the blond receptionist to hear.

"I'll carry the books in there and then I'll find Gran." Kellan signed the register after she did, his signature indecipherable. But she liked it.

At the threshold, Paige paused to scan the room for her great-aunt. Not by the window, nor the plush beige couch or flanking the fireplace. Ah. In the corner, tucked into a cozy conversation with another lady. "There she is."

"What do you know, she's with Gran." Kellan's brows lifted in surprise. "I didn't know they knew one another."

"Marigold told me they're all in a knitting circle together." Paige couldn't contain herself and rushed across the lounge. "Aunt Trudie?"

Aunt Trudie and Kellan's grandma hopped to their feet at the same time and grinned, but that was the only similarity the women shared. Aunt Trudie's salt-and-pepper hair fell past her shoulders, draping down the back of her earth-toned bohemian garb. Kellan's blue-eyed grandma, however, kept her steel-gray curls short and wore hot pink lipstick and a matching blouse.

"Paigey." Aunt Trudie embraced her in a fierce hug. "So good to see you."

"I'm glad to see you, too." She melted into the hug and let her aunt's affection seep into her bones. *I needed this, didn't I, Lord?*

When they broke apart, Paige extended her hand to Kellan's grandma. "Hi. I'm Paige."

"Eileen Lambert."

Now Paige saw where Kellan got that charming smile.

Paige gestured at the paper sacks Kellan had set down on the table. "We brought books for you to read, share, keep, give, whatever you want."

"*You* brought," Kellan corrected with a mock glare.

"Actually, it was *you*." Paige leveled him with a look of her own, which wasn't easy to do, considering he was over half a foot taller than she. "You donated them."

"The store did, not me. And it was *your* idea." There was his charming Lambert smile again.

"They're from both of you, then?" Aunt Trudie examined the contents of the paper sacks. "These will get a lot of use around here, won't they, Eileen?"

"I'll say. Thanks, you two."

"So Trudie tells me you've moved to town, Paige." Eileen tucked her purple knitting project into a maroon brocade bag.

"Not exactly." Paige had already informed Aunt Trudie that she would be staying in Widow's Peak Creek for a while, but she hadn't elaborated on the details. Trudie hadn't pried, either, but Paige now felt she owed her great-aunt a fuller explanation. Eileen would indubitably find out, anyway, so she shared with both of them about her broken engagement, lack of job and the end of her semester's classes, allowing her the flexibility to take time to regroup. She didn't mention Peanut, though.

"Poor thing," Eileen murmured, rubbing Paige's arm. "I'm sorry your relationship didn't work out."

"Thanks, but it's for the best." Paige didn't have to fake a smile when she said it, either. God had saved her from being married to Mr. Wrong. He'd turned out to be Mr. Sneaky And Mean, in fact. How could she be upset about being spared from a life with him?

Eileen took Kellan's elbow. "What do you say we leave these gals to chat and take a brisk walk in the garden, sweetheart?"

"Sounds great." Kellan's nod for Paige was encouraging as he escorted his grandma out of the lounge.

Paige sat down in Eileen's vacated spot. "How are you, Aunt Trudie?"

"Fine as a frog hair, but there's more going on with you than a broken engagement." Her gemstone-bead necklace swung wide as she leaned closer. "I felt the bump when we hugged, Paigey. You're expecting."

Paige looked down at her unpolished nails. She'd known she'd have to tell Aunt Trudie the truth at some point, but not like this.

Maybe it was best to rip the Band-Aid off, as it were. Soon, she'd be showing enough that everyone would know. Mickey, Marigold, Kellan's grandma Eileen, everyone she encountered. They might judge her because she wasn't married, which sent fear skittering through her veins. But all she could do was trust God.

She met Aunt Trudie's hazel gaze. "I'm five months along. Aidan, the father, gave up his parental rights."

"Oh, Paigey. How awful for you." Aunt Trudie's bony hand landed atop hers.

"You should know, I haven't told Mom about the baby yet."

"Oh?" Aunt Trudie's thin eyebrows rose.

"She'll want answers I don't have right now, and you know how she is about wanting me to have all my ducks in a row. I don't know when I'll finish school now, or where to live, or when I'll be able to start teaching preschool, but I know God will help me. I started going to church—"

"Well, hallelujah!" Trudie clapped.

"Thanks. Yeah. My life's different now, for sure. But that doesn't mean raising this baby alone will be easy. I know that, but I'll do whatever it takes for him or her to have a good life."

"Of course you will. You're a good mother already."

"I don't know about that." What sort of mother didn't know where her baby would be born? Nor did she know much about infant care. Preschoolers, sure, but newborns?

No way.

"Part of being a mother is taking care of yourself so you have strength and grace for your child." Aunt Trudie sat back in her chair. "You did the right thing, coming to Widow's Peak Creek, among people who love you."

What a funny thing to say. Aunt Trudie was the only person in town who loved her.

But maybe it wasn't the number of people that mattered. Maybe it was the love itself that counted. Now that she thought about it, though, Paige recognized a yearning for others to be part of Peanut's life. To care about him or her. As if in response, the baby nudged her, and Paige made her first decision when it came to the plan she had to put into place.

She'd chased love and settled for fool's gold. But with God's help, she'd raise the baby in a place where he or she was well loved, not just by her, but by others, too. Family or friends, whichever God allowed her. Wherever it was.

He'd show her the place when she came to it.

Chapter Five

After kissing Gran goodbye, Kellan paused in the lobby, hands stuffed into the pockets of his olive chinos. Should he wait for Paige to finish up? He wanted to be a support to her, but at the same time, he didn't want to intrude on her privacy. Judging by what he could see of Paige's face through the glass lobby doors, Paige and Trudie were clearly having an intense conversation.

Before he could decide whether to stay or go, Paige hugged Trudie and hurried toward him, her eyes bright as if full of unshed tears.

Uh-oh. He opened the door for her. "How'd your visit go?"

She waited until they were outside the lobby, in the fading light of early evening, to smile up at him. "Wonderful. Surprising, too. She could tell I'm pregnant by hugging me. I didn't expect her to find out that way, but she was supportive and loving."

"So you're okay?" He watched her while she dug her car keys from her purse.

"I'm fine. Super fine." The overhead streetlights flickered on, and she turned her smile up at them as if they'd come on just for her. "I hope you had a good visit, too."

"I did. Had a nice talk with Gran." He waited for her to unlock her car and get inside. "Good night, Paige."

"Good night."

He let her pull out of the parking lot first so he could follow her home.

His hands clutched the steering wheel the entire way.

Paige might be fine after their visit to Creekside, but he wasn't.

There was a reason he didn't visit Gran as often as she deserved. Why he'd tensed up the moment he crossed the threshold of the facility.

One whiff of the bleachy, disinfectant smell used in places like that, and it felt like he'd traveled back four years in time to the trauma hospital at Bagram Air Base. He'd been taken there after the ambush on his squad, treated for a gunshot wound to his thigh while he lay in a hospital cot grappling with the horror of Drew's death.

It may have been four years since that day, but it was a fresh wound in his gut every time he went back to that moment. Because Drew Faraday would still be alive if it hadn't been for Kellan's poor judgment.

Living with the guilt of it every day was bad enough. But when he was triggered by that industrial cleaner smell?

It took him back to Bagram, and it was all brand-new.

He hated it, hated himself for the weakness that kept him from visiting Gran. Sure, he spent time with her. He saw her at church and picked her up for the occasional lunch out, but he hadn't met her at her condo or inside the Creekside lounge in ages.

Today he'd wanted to go along with Paige, though. Wanted to see Gran. Figured it wouldn't be so bad.

But it was obvious by the bleach smell that the lobby had just been mopped. Faking a calm demeanor took all he had. Five seconds of bickering with Paige over who brought the books had helped, but Gran's suggestion of a walk was a blessing. The fresh air and her steady stream of chatter enabled him to breathe deeply, pray and bring his pulse down to a regular rhythm.

Coming back inside to tell Gran goodbye,

though? He'd had to stuff his hands in his pockets to hide the shaking in his fingers.

Even now as he entered his house, his hands still trembled. Gladys and Jet didn't seem to care when he patted them, though. "Thanks, guys."

When will this end, Lord? What more must I do to make up for—

He had to just stop and quit questioning God's timing, or he'd be plagued with nightmares, if he actually fell asleep tonight.

He had to shift gears. Literally.

Two hours' hard bicycle ride later, Kellan's legs and lungs ached, but his brain was numb—as he'd hoped. He would have stayed out later, but he didn't like riding after dark, despite his reflective cycling clothes and the lights on his bike. So once the sun went down, he headed home.

Besides, he'd worn himself out. That was all he'd wanted to do in the first place.

Turning into his driveway, he zipped to the side of the garage door. Straddling the mountain bike, he dug for his keys, only for his cell phone to buzz with a text from his pocket. Something with the shop? Or maybe it was Benton, his pastor, or one of the other guys in his Wednesday morning breakfast Bible study group.

Nope. His stepdad Don's name was on the screen.

Any profit information from Saturday's book signing? What kind of numbers are we talking about?

Don was nothing if not to the point. And predictably concerned with money.

The store's primary focus was a source of contention between the two of them. Kellan wanted to make enough to get by and engage in the community, but Don's latest goal required more capital. He wanted enough to open a second bookstore in the nearby town of Pinehurst.

The text could've waited until morning, when Kellan was at the store and could access their accounting program. Don must be working something up. Probably to do with opening a second store. The matter shouldn't bother him this much, but Kellan's muscles tightened, threatening to undo all the stress relief he'd just put in.

Kellan tapped out a response with his thumbs.

Looked good. I'll get numbers to you later.

The reply was immediate.

We need more of these events if we're going to expand.

"But I don't want to expand," he said aloud as if Don could hear him through text.

"Kellan?"

He turned at the soft voice. Paige pattered down the driveway, her flip-flop sandals slapping in rhythm. The security lights in his yard illuminated a foil-wrapped package in her hand. "You cycle a lot, huh?"

Phew, she hadn't seemed to overhear his aggravated response to Don. "Every day when I can, but at least on weekends. Alone or with the local cycling club." He took off his helmet and wiped sweat from his brow with the back of his wrist. "What's that you've got there?"

"My bananas all turned brown overnight and I bake when I'm worried, so, ta-da!" Her laugh trilled through the evening air. "Do you like banana nut bread?"

"I love banana nut bread." He climbed off the bike and propped it against the garage, balancing his helmet on a handlebar. "I don't like hearing you're worried, though. You were happy when we left Creekside. Did something happen?"

"I got a text from someone in one of my education classes telling me all about her new aide job, and how close she is to getting credentialed."

And Paige's credentialing process had been

put on hold, for who knew how long. Seemed like he wasn't the only one set off by an innocent text tonight. "I'm sure, knowing you, you're happy for your friend. But I'm guessing she's where you thought you'd be right now. And that stings."

"Exactly. I'm not jealous, honest. I'm happy for her. But at the same time, I felt bad about myself. For being in my situation, and for feeling…upset that I'm not where she is. All the trust I had in God's timing went out the window. What's wrong with me? I really thought I trusted God."

"Nothing's wrong, Paige. I've been walking with Jesus for a few years now, but that doesn't mean I'm immune to things causing me anxiety or frustration. The good thing about it is it keeps me turning toward God. Listening for Him."

"Right now the only voice I hear is my mom's, in my head, saying it could've been me within weeks of being credentialed. It *should've* been me." She stared, unfocused, at the sweetgum tree. "I had an overwhelming urge to figure out my future right that second. But then I realized, in forcing decisions that I'm clearly not ready to make, I didn't trust God in that moment. I felt—I feel—my failure in that as heavily as I do the failure of my past choices."

He wished he could tell her that the past didn't define them, but it sure did him. All he could do was share his experience. "I know it's not my business, Paige, but I think you're better off waiting for God's plan to unfold, rather than jumping ahead without Him. That said, I wish trusting God was a onetime decision, but I find that it's a moment-by-moment choice sometimes. For me, anyway."

And right now he needed to choose to trust again.

She bit her lip. "After reading that text, I felt so petty and envious, but you make me feel like I can tell you things. You don't judge me, and I appreciate that."

"I'm in no position to judge you, Paige." For a whole host of reasons.

"Most people don't see the world like that, but I'm glad you do." In the glow of the streetlights, her eyes darkened to liquid ink. As a smile stretched her lips, he felt something shift in his chest. He felt drawn to her, like—

Nope. He was not going to finish that sentence.

Being drawn like that led to attraction. Which led to emotional connection, which led nowhere but trouble.

There were a hundred reasons why he couldn't develop an emotional connection to Paige. She'd come to him to help. He was her boss. Those two alone were giant red flags.

There was also that fact that Kellan was responsible for her brother's death, and he'd been keeping it a secret from Paige and her mom for four years.

No, she was the worst person in the world to be drawn to.

Desperate to look somewhere else, he peeled back a corner of foil and took a deep whiff. Nutty and sweet. Instantly, his stomach rumbled, reminding him he hadn't eaten dinner. "I may have to eat this the minute I get inside."

"Slather it with butter." She rubbed her stomach, just over the bump. "Sooo good that way."

"I'll definitely do that. Thank you."

"I baked Marigold some, too. I'd better take it to her." She stepped backward up the drive. "Good night."

"Good night." Kellan unlocked the garage and shoved his bike in its place. Once he was back inside the house, he greeted Jet, Gladys and Frank, who all showed him their affection in their unique ways. Then he nipped off a corner of the warm banana bread and popped it into his mouth. Wow.

He didn't know much, when it came to his brokenness or guilt or even how to help a pregnant woman in need, but one thing he knew. Well, two.

One, this was the best banana bread he'd ever eaten in nearly twenty-nine years of existence.

And two? Being around Paige Faraday was pretty nice. He just had to be careful not to think of her as anything beyond Drew's sister. A friend.

Anything beyond that was impossible. Not just with her, but with anyone. After all he'd done, he didn't deserve to be happy. Ever.

The next three days passed in a busy blur at Open Book for Paige, a pleasant distraction from her internal wrestling matches. After talking to Kellan on the driveway, she'd renewed her intention to rely on God, and not forge a plan that might not be in His will.

That meant time. And trust.

At least she had a beautiful place to do that, and a job where she could be around nice people. Like the tall, ginger-haired woman who approached the check-out counter with a smile and a handful of children's paperbacks.

"All ready?" Paige reached across the counter for the books. Half of the slender volumes were on knights, and the other half were on pioneers. "Ooh, someone must be interested in history."

"I'm trying to expose them to different time periods." *They* must be the woman's children.

"I love it. And if you're ever interested in local history, there are some good titles over there for kids of all ages." She tipped her head toward the bookshelf by the museum display in the front of the store.

"Really? Hang on, is it too late for me to look? You haven't finished ringing me up, have you?"

"Not at all." There wasn't anyone else in line, so Paige left the register alone while the woman dashed to peruse the bookshelf.

Now that she'd worked at Open Book for a few days, Paige was starting to feel more comfortable with the processes. While the store and its wares were interesting, though, it was the people she'd enjoyed the most. Aside from Kellan, who was his usual helpful, handsome self—not that she was dwelling on his handsomeness, of course—the few other employees were kind.

Likewise, the customers were friendly and interesting. Yesterday she'd helped Mickey read to the little kids who came for weekly

Toddler Story Time, held upstairs in the kids' section.

And she'd also already grown fond of Herb Parkman, the wrinkled fellow who came every morning for the free coffee. He never bought anything, and usually left by lunch, but he'd stuck around today, rooted to the comfy chair in the magazine section. Which reminded her, she had tucked a brown paper bag under the counter for a quiet moment. "I brought you something, Herb."

He looked up from his *National Geographic* while she handed him the bag. "I've been in a baking frenzy and brought you some muffins. Banana nut."

"Thanks." A single word, but more than she'd heard him utter to this point. He set down the magazine and dug into the bag.

She would've talked more but the redhead returned from the other side of the shelf, three books in hand. Paige hurried back around the counter to take the books, all illustrated accounts of life in a gold rush town during the 1850s.

"I had no idea these were there."

"We just moved them from upstairs." Paige gave her the total. "I hope your kids enjoy the books."

"Oh, they will. Thanks for the tip."

"Have a great day." Paige's gaze followed the woman out the door and through the front window as she passed, until she'd gone far enough that the bookshelf blocked Paige's view.

"Everything okay?" Kellan's voice drew her around. "You've got an interesting look on your face I can't figure out."

She hadn't heard him come out of the office. "I used to tell my preschoolers that it's my thinking face."

"Something's on your mind, then?"

Paige hesitated. She'd worked here four days as a temporary hire. What did she know about the bookselling business? Or any retail business for that matter?

But he'd asked. "It's the museum display."

He grabbed a file from behind the counter. "What about it?"

"It's not working."

"What do you mean, not working? No one looks at it?" His brows met. "Are you suggesting I get rid of it? Because it's part of the building's heritage."

"I'm not saying to chuck the blacksmith display. No way. But no one looks at it, and as far as I'm aware, we aren't selling any of the books displayed by it. At least, not until five minutes ago when I suggested them to a customer. School's out for the summer. We've had plenty of tourists. One of them should've bought something by now."

Herb wasn't even pretending to read the *National Geographic* anymore. He stared at them, chewing on a muffin.

Kellan leaned against the counter. "You think tourists aren't interested in history?"

"It's more that I don't think anyone knows that stuff is there. In fact, I didn't see it until you showed me. I'd totally missed it because the bookshelf hides it."

There. She'd said it. Hopefully, he didn't fire her.

Instead, he rubbed the faint stubble on his chiseled chin. "Faith and I envisioned the display as a nook, visible from the street. But you've got a point about it being closed off. I'll move the shelf, and let's see how sales go. Good idea, Paige."

His words sounded boss-like, but his smile? He didn't intend it to, but it did funny things to her leg bones. She really had to get a grip on that reaction. It was hard, though, the way he kept smiling at her, and she didn't dare break eye contact. It had been like this between them Monday night, too, when she'd brought him banana bread. She'd felt like they could talk about all kinds of things. Anything and everything. Or not talk at all—

"Ahem." Herb stared at them, holding up his coffee cup.

Phew. She was no longer transfixed by Kellan's super-powered smile anymore. *Thanks for the interruption, Lord.* "Down to the dregs, Herb?"

Herb, man of few words that he was, didn't answer. He didn't need to, though. She moved around the counter to fetch his empty cup. "We can't have that, can we? I'll brew some more in the back—"

She broke off as something snapped in her side, like nothing she'd ever experienced before.

Kellan's sideways glance turned into a double take. "Paige? Are you okay?"

She didn't know. "It's a…twinge."

"A twinge?"

Actually, it was more than a twinge now that she'd said it. Pain speared into the right half of her midsection. She grabbed the counter for support.

"A kick." It wasn't a question as Kellan came up beside her.

"Not a kick." Peanut wasn't dancing. *Please no, God. Please don't let anything be wrong with the baby.*

"Who's your doctor in town?"

"I don't—have one yet." Stupid, stupid. "I

thought I had time to pick a doctor. I'm so far away from my due date."

"Sarah Graves is my cousin, and an OB/ GYN," Mickey said. When did she get here? Paige glanced up to see Mickey and Herb, magazine in hand, gathered around the counter, where Paige still clung on for dear life. Mickey reached for the store phone. "I can call her, if you want."

I don't want this at all. Paige's gaze fixed on the hardwood floor as a fresh stab of pain pierced her side.

"Paige." Kellan bent his knees so his face was close enough to whisper, level with hers, and she had no choice but to look into his blue gaze. "Is it insurance you're worried about? Because I'll—"

"I've got insurance." She was a saver and a planner. But that didn't mean she'd expected to need it just yet. She wiped moisture from her cheeks. When had she started crying? "Thank you, Mickey. That would be helpful."

Within two minutes she was buckled into the passenger seat of Kellan's truck, crossing the narrow bridge over the creek and heading south. Paige shifted, extending one leg, as the pain subsided enough for her to take a deep breath. "It's going away. I think."

"But not gone?" He glanced at her.

The twinge in her side made itself known again. "Not quite."

"I know you're scared. I'm kinda scared, too."

His admission unleashed a wave of adrenaline through her. "Nobody planned for this baby, but I love it so much, Kellan. I can't… I don't want anything to happen to it."

"Hey." Driving with his left hand, he reached for her with his right. His hand was warm and solid atop hers. "Let's pray, okay?"

While he drove, he asked God to protect her and the baby, thanking God for modern medicine and the proximity of Mickey's cousin's office.

"And thanks for Kellan driving me. Amen," she tacked on at the end, through her sniffles.

"Of course, Paige." He squeezed her fingers.

Maybe it wasn't appropriate, but in the waiting room, she didn't let go of his hand until she was called into an examination room.

While she sat on the exam table waiting for Dr. Graves, she prayed, but her thoughts kept flitting to Kellan. He'd been kind to sit with her out in the waiting room. Now that she was in the examination room, he'd surely gone back to work. There was no reason for him to stay. It wasn't like he was the baby's father.

The thought stopped her cold.

Kellan had done more for her and Peanut than Aidan ever would do.

She didn't know Kellan well, but he'd never abandon his child, or his child's mother. What would it have been like to have ended up with a man like Kellan? One she could count on?

She'd never know, so it was no use dwelling on such a question. She had decided to raise Peanut on her own, so the baby would never suffer the grief of attaching to someone, only for them to step away. She renewed that intention to herself now.

She'd protect Peanut with everything she had. Her hands cradled her tummy as if she could will the baby to believe her promise.

Chapter Six

Every time the door to the examination rooms opened, Kellan rose to his feet and— —nope, it wouldn't be Paige. He was up and down like a prairie dog, his system so full of adrenaline that he could probably run a marathon in record time.

It didn't help his agitated state of mind that he was sitting in a medical office, either. The smell of industrial cleaners was too faint to send him back to Bagram, thankfully, but that didn't mean it wasn't on his mind. The vinyl-upholstered chairs, murmured talk about insurance cards and the wall-mounted television tuned in to the garden channel brought to mind the weeks of physical therapy sessions he endured after the incident in Afghanistan.

The gunshot wound he'd sustained didn't bother him much at all now. If only his memories could heal, as well.

But this was not the time to think about any of that. He should do his best to relax, for the sake of all the people in the waiting room with him who kept darting suspicious looks his way. Nevertheless, he wanted to be ready the instant Paige emerged from the examination rooms.

If she emerged. What if they'd taken her to the hospital in an ambulance?

His stomach swooped low. All he could do was pray. And if it took much longer, he'd ask the receptionist for details.

"Paige?" He hopped up when she came through the door, her head down as she dug through her purse.

Her lips parted in a surprised smile. A smile had to mean good news, right? "You're still here?"

Where else would he be? "Are you okay? Should you be sitting down?" He scanned the room for a wheelchair so he could push her out to the truck.

"I'm fine. So is the baby." Her smile widened, making her eyes crinkle.

Relief flooded him, sinking deep into his bones. "Thank God."

They'd parked close to the door, so in moments they were sitting in the hot truck cab. First order of business, cooling things down.

He started the engine and lowered the windows so they wouldn't roast on the way back.

Paige shoved a white rectangle of slick photographic paper under his nose. He blinked at the black-and-white image. He couldn't tell one curvy part from another, but he knew what it was, and it made his breath catch. "That's the baby."

"A profile shot. Here's Peanut's head." She traced a circle. She couldn't tear her gaze away from the tiny nub of a...nose?

Wow. That was the baby's nose!

"Peanut's really okay, then?"

"Perfect heartbeat, perfect growth. Unfortunately, Peanut didn't cooperate when we tried to find out if it's a boy or girl, but I don't care. He or she is fine and so am I."

"What about the pain? You were white-knuckled there for a while."

"The pain was—well, it was probably some ligaments. I hope it's not too much personal information, but now you know it's nothing big."

Any joy he felt evaporated. "I've pushed you so hard at Open Book your ligaments are injured."

"They're not injured. What I experienced isn't unheard of, according to Dr. Graves." She tucked the photo lovingly into her purse. "But

I didn't know that, so I'm so grateful you got me here so fast."

He pulled out into traffic, his tension lessening. "My pleasure. Really."

"Ha," she barked. "Everyone just lo-oves to sit in waiting rooms."

He almost argued that he wasn't going to leave her alone, but something held him back, like an invisible finger on his lips. If he hadn't stayed with her, who would have? Not her good-for-nothing ex-fiancé.

It was a heavy topic, though, and he didn't want to wipe the pretty smile from her face. So he continued on with her teasing mood and grunted. "Are you kidding? First time I've sat down all day. My feet were killing me."

"Glad I could provide a break for you, then." She shook her head at the nonsense of it.

"It was pretty comfortable in there. Nice chairs."

"They're extra-squishy to accommodate pregnant people."

He hadn't noticed that. "Really?"

"No. They're regular chairs." She gave his arm a playful slap.

His arm felt weird where she'd touched it. It didn't hurt, of course. The slap was more of a tap. But it almost burned. Or froze, giving him goose pimples.

Paige was not being flirtatious, though. She was relieved and happy. What was wrong with him, reacting like this? *She's Drew's pregnant sister, and you are a mess of a man, Lambert.*

He rubbed his arm. "I'll drop you off at your car, if you're okay to drive home."

"There's an hour left on my shift."

"No need, Paige."

"Dr. Graves said I can work. And I want to."

He'd feel a lot better if she went home and rested, but he would never presume to know what was best for her. "Just know your health comes first. If you feel at all concerned or tired, today or any other day, I don't want you to worry about your job. It's there no matter what." He'd made the moment heavy, which was probably not what she needed, so he took a breath. "Okay, speech over."

"Thank you, Kellan. If I thank you a million times for everything you've done to help me, it wouldn't be enough."

"Seriously, do not thank me." He wasn't doing anything any normal person wouldn't do. Besides, he owed her. He owed Drew. His final words to Drew, there in the desert, were a promise to help Paige and her mom however he could.

Even if she'd never know the real reason

why. That he'd trusted the wrong person. That he'd been the one who was supposed to die—

"What kind of car does Herb drive?" Her peppy tone drew him to the present as he pulled into the parking lot around the corner from the bookstore.

"Herb walks here. Why?"

"I wondered if he's still here. He looked worried and I want him to know everything's okay. Maybe I should bake him some more banana bread, too."

"More?"

"Yeah, I gave him some muffins."

"That must have made his day."

Her grin was cheeky. "I'm not sure. He didn't say anything."

"I'd have been shocked if he did." Once she was out of the truck, he locked the doors and they walked around the building to the front door. "Don't overdo it, Paige. Banana bread or work. You've put in a full day, had a doctor's appointment and come up with a fantastic marketing idea for the store, and all I have to do is move a bookshelf."

"So my idea was good?"

Something about the way she said it sounded fishy. "Yes."

"Good, because I have another one. But I'll keep it to myself if you don't want to hear it."

She mimed locking her lips shut and throwing away the key.

"Why wouldn't I want to hear it?"

As they rounded the corner to the bookstore entrance, she touched his forearm. Less like she was holding him back than she had grave news to deliver. "No offense, but I think we need to revamp the kids' section."

"Seriously?" He'd spent hours freestyle painting the Dr. Seuss quotes on the staircase. "What's wrong with it?"

"It's cramped. I helped with Toddler Story Time yesterday, and we need more room."

"They're toddlers. How much room do they need?" He grinned so she knew he was teasing.

"More," she teased back. "It's summer, so older siblings attended, too. More kids means more parents, and you should see those poor moms and dads, crammed against shelves and trying to stay out of the way. All we need to do is move a few shelves back."

"Consider it done."

"Thanks, but I was also thinking…you should consider selling educational toys. As a complement to the books, not in place of them. Like puppets and stuff like that. I think they'd sell, especially if we display them in an eye-catching way. There's not a focal point up there, so I think a painted piece of furniture, like an armoire with the doors removed, would be a good way to go. We could get one pretty inexpensively."

She'd put a lot of thought into this, hadn't she? Through to an armoire. "Spend money to make money, right? I'll see if Faith has anything at her antiques store that might work."

"I'm not done." She took a comically large breath as they entered Open Book. "We should order a new rug. Trust me on this one."

Hmm. Don wouldn't go on trust. "I might need a little more to go on here."

"That old thing up there isn't non-skid, for one thing. Oh, hello." Paige turned her grin toward a couple standing by the register. "Have you been helped?"

Kellan's smile fell along with his spirits. Not that he wasn't happy to see the well-dressed woman with chin-length blond curls or the balding man beside her with black-rimmed glasses, but lately, whenever they'd visited, there had been tension. "Paige, meet Belinda and Don Phelps. My mom and stepdad."

"Wow, so nice to meet you." Paige thrust out her hand.

Mom grinned so wide you could see her back teeth. "Paige Faraday? We've heard so much about you."

"From Kellan?" Paige's head tipped to the side.

"From his grandma Eileen, actually. My late husband's mother. We're quite close." Mom still clutched Paige's hand. "Kellan is a *closed book* when it comes to his personal life. Not like the name of his store. Get it?"

Since when was Mom a comedian?

"So what brings you two to town?" Kellan intruded before things got weirder.

"We live outside San Francisco," Mom explained to Paige, finally releasing her hand so she could tuck an errant curl behind her ear. "But every once in a while we fancy a day trip to see Kellan."

"And the store," Don added, scanning the place as if searching out dust motes.

"Don's my business partner," Kellan told Paige.

"Were you two out for a walk?" Mom's eyes sparkled.

"An errand," he answered before Paige did, in part to protect her privacy about the doctor's appointment, and in part to disabuse his mother of any romantic notions she was harboring. And she was clearly harboring them, the way she kept looking at Paige and lifting her shoulders as if she was tickled the proverbial shade of pink.

"I'll let you folks visit, but it was so nice to meet you." Paige shook hands with them both.

Kellan escorted Don and his mom to the office and shut the door behind him. He didn't want anyone, especially Paige, to overhear what his mom was undoubtedly going to say.

"Yep, everything's okay." Paige kept her voice low as she explained her pain, and her pregnancy, to Mickey, even though there weren't any customers in the store this close to closing time. "I'm sorry to have caused such a fuss."

"You did no such thing. We all care about you. Even Herb was worried. He thought it was your appendix, though."

"I missed hearing Herb speak a complete sentence." Paige chuckled. "I'll fill him in tomorrow. Maybe I'd better bake more muffins tonight."

"We all might need the pick-me-up." Mickey glanced at the door beneath the staircase. "Don Phelps tends not to leave Kellan in the best of moods lately."

Paige pulled out one of the dust rags they kept behind the counter and wiped down the nearest bookshelf. "Kellan said they're business partners?"

Mickey copied her, dusting another shelf. "I've worked here since the beginning, when

Don and Kellan started Open Book. Don owns stakes in several businesses in town, and that's how he and Kellan teamed up. It didn't take long for Don to meet Belinda and for them to start dating. Since they got married, though, Don became a lot more vocal about things he wants changed at the store, and he and Kellan don't see things quite the same way. In fact, I think Don has plans."

"Plans for what? I feel bad now, dumping my ideas on him."

"Ideas?"

"To move that shelf." She pointed at the one blocking the anvil from view. "Sell educational toys. Get a new rug upstairs for Toddler Story Time."

Mickey laughed. "Kellan won't mind that. Especially not coming from you."

As opposed to a suggestion from Don? Made sense, if there was tension in their relationship.

But something about the way Mickey was smiling as she dusted made Paige think twice. Surely, Mickey didn't mean Kellan—

No, that was preposterous.

She turned her back on Mickey so she wouldn't see that smile anymore.

Don toggled through programs on Kellan's computer, shaking his head. "Running errands with employees, Kel? Doesn't seem like a productive use of her work hours."

"Don." Mom's voice was a snap. "*That's* the girl Eileen told me about."

Kellan had to cut down his mom's expectations right now, before she got carried away. "I'm not sure what Gran said, Mom, but Paige works here now. She's Drew Faraday's sister." Not that his mom knew anything more about Drew's death than that he was killed the same night Kellan was shot in the leg.

"I know who she is. And it's not what Eileen said, but what you did. You and Paige visited Creekside together."

"Her aunt lives there. She had an idea to donate books, and we went over after work Monday."

"You make it sound so impersonal. But neither Eileen nor I are fooled, sweetheart." Mom looked like she was about to clap. "It's about time you got a girlfriend."

The ache in Kellan's head spread to his scalp. Mom had been pushing him to get married, or at least go on a date, since he'd come home from Afghanistan. He hated to disappoint her, but it wasn't like she'd never be a mother-in-law or grandma. Kellan's younger sister in New York would get married one of these days.

"Stop right there, Mom. We are not dating."

"Not yet, maybe. You two looked awfully chummy just now."

"We were discussing her ideas to update the kids' section." The office felt cramped all of a sudden. Not that it was huge to begin with, but there was ample space for two computer-topped desks, a conference table, filing cabinets, a copy machine and some folding chairs. Right now it felt downright claustrophobic, though, and Kellan wished his mom would stop smirking. "There's nothing going on."

"Is it because she's pregnant?"

How did she find out? "Mom, that's her business."

"I can tell by looking at her, though. So could Eileen, so don't gape like that."

Who knew about Peanut and who didn't wasn't the point, though. "Her baby has nothing to do with it."

"Of course not, but you're bound to be concerned about the role of the baby's father in her life." She perched on the desk perpendicular to the larger one where Don sat, perusing the accounting program on the computer. "It's workable, though, honey. It shouldn't necessarily be a barrier to you moving on from this 'staying single' phase of yours."

"It's not a phase." The topic of his mom

wanting him to get married was as stale as old bread. "And not that it's any of our business, but Paige is not interested in a relationship. She's here in Widow's Peak Creek to regroup, and I'm going to honor that. Just like I'm not going to cross the boss-employee line."

"Smart," Don said as he scrolled through the accounts.

Mom's eager expression crumpled. "But she won't work here forever, and I can tell you like her."

"We're friends."

"Not like you're friends with Benton or any of your bicycle friends. You had a gooshy look on your face with Paige. Are you making excuses because of your PTSD? It's nothing to be ashamed of, sweetheart."

"I agree with you on that, but I do not have post-traumatic stress disorder."

Not a severe case, anyway. He'd spoken to a counselor when he was still in the military, sharing his response to triggers like smells as well as his role in Drew's death. The counselor offered suggestions, but also expressed his opinion that Kellan was able to function well enough to move on with his life. What happened in Afghanistan wasn't really his fault, after all.

Except it was. No one seemed to understand

that. He didn't deserve to feel better about the night Drew died, to "move on" without guilt. And he definitely wouldn't bring a woman into his torment.

He'd told God as much. Not that his family understood his conversations with God, either, since they didn't go to church.

Don turned around in the swivel chair to level Kellan with an exasperated look. "Are you two done with the dating talk?"

"Yes," Kellan answered over his mom's annoyed sniff. "What's up, Don?"

"Pinehurst. A second store. Here's what I'm thinking."

Kellan was actually happy to talk about the prospect, even though he didn't want to do it. The topic was far preferable to talking to his mother about a romantic relationship with Paige.

He hated to disappoint his mom, but he'd be single forever, and she needed to accept it and move on.

Chapter Seven

Paige stopped by the store and picked up two cans of pumpkin puree on the way home, and before dark fell, she had a warm, foil-wrapped loaf in hand for Kellan. Jet and Gladys played in the backyard, hurrying to the fence to greet her.

"Hi, guys. Where's your human?" She walked along the fence toward Kellan's front door.

"He's out riding, dear Paige," Marigold shouted from her porch, where she sat on a wicker chair.

"I didn't see you there." She was sorry to have missed Kellan, but she'd planned on giving Marigold a loaf of bread, anyway. She altered course to Marigold's porch. "Then this has your name on it."

"Ooh. What a treat." Marigold accepted the

loaf, and the two of them visited for a half hour before the streetlights flickered on Kellan hadn't returned, and Paige couldn't help the knot of disappointment forming in her stomach.

A silly reaction, considering she'd see him in the morning.

She had his loaf ready, as well as miniature loaves for Mickey and Herb, baked in pans she borrowed from Marigold. She arrived at Open Book a few minutes early the next morning so she could pass them out, and the weird knot in her stomach loosened the moment she saw Kellan in the office. He stared at a file, his hair stylishly messy.

What was that knot about, anyway? She wasn't worried about him, was she? Or had she just been anxious to see him?

Neither of those were warranted, so she shoved away the thought and knocked on the open door.

He looked up and smiled. "Hey."

"Hey. Sorry to interrupt, but I brought you a snack. Or lunch. Whatever you do with it is your business."

He made a show of rubbing his stomach. "Banana nut bread."

"Pumpkin this time." She set it on the smaller of the two desks. "I tried to give it to you last night, but Marigold said you were out for a ride."

"Yeah. Good stress relief. My relationship with Mom and Don isn't always the easiest, and I needed to clear my head." He shook his head as if shaking away the past evening. "But I almost knocked on your door, too."

Her heart skipped a beat. "Why didn't you?"

"I figured you might be tired after yesterday. The pain and all that."

"I'm fine. But I'm sorry you have a tough time with your folks on occasion."

"My mom's heart is in the right place."

"My mom's is, too, I guess." She leaned against the desk by the bread. "But she's going to be so disappointed in me when she learns about Peanut. I'm twenty-four, haven't completed my education and I'm unsure where to go from here. A failure, in her book."

"For what it's worth, I admire your perseverance. Doing what you think is best." His blue eyes widened. "I don't know why I didn't think of this before, but you said you only have, what, two classes left? Is it possible to finish them before the baby comes?"

"In theory, yes, but I'd have to enroll right now for summer session. I'd have to move from Widow's Peak Creek to a town with a college."

The thought of leaving town right now made her stomach ache.

"You wouldn't necessarily have to leave town if you took courses online, would you?"

Oh! "If they're offered online. I don't know why I haven't thought to look before."

Before she could blink, he dropped into the swivel chair in front of the computer, typing something into a search engine. A college website appeared on the screen. He placed the cursor in its search bar and then rose, gesturing for her to take his seat. "This is the school Mickey attends, online, anyway. Maybe they offer what you need."

"Curriculum for Early Childhood," she said as she typed. "Wow, there it is." It was listed as an intensive summer online course. "It's concentrated, but doable. Let me try the other one." She typed in Family and Community for Early Childhood.

It, too, was available online in the shorter format. She could be finished with both courses by midsummer, well before Peanut was born. Beyond work, cooking, reading and walking to the park for exercise, she didn't have anything going on that would interfere with homework. Definitely no social life. She clicked on the box labeled "tuition" and gasped.

"What's wrong?" He leaned over her chair

to better view the monitor, smelling faintly of citrusy aftershave. So deliciously citrusy that she had to force herself not to turn toward him and inhale again.

"Nothing's wrong." Except how weird she was being with him this close to her. "I'm just shocked by the cost, unless this price per unit is a typo in my favor."

His forefinger tapped the price per unit on the screen, his biceps bulging right in her line of sight. Boss or no boss, it was impossible to ignore the effect Kellan had on her. Had always had on her, since they met when Drew was alive and he'd almost knocked her flat with his smile.

But she'd been careful not to allow her thoughts to run off in a direction beyond an objective acknowledgment that he was an attractive man, inside and out. End of story.

She needed to buckle down on that resolution now.

It helped her resolve when he shifted out of the range of her vision. "Mickey told me this place is as reputable as it is affordable."

She snapped to attention. Oh, yes, they were talking about school. She did mental calculations in her head, grateful she'd always had a habit of squirreling away her paychecks so she could pad her savings account. "I can do this."

She spun on the swivel chair to share her excitement, and smacked right into him, her nose ramming his neck.

She hopped up, hand over her mouth. "I'm so sorry. I thought you'd moved back." Instead, he'd bent over to look at the monitor with her.

"No, I shouldn't have been that close." He waved it off.

"But I plowed into you." And something shimmery and peach splotched his pale blue collar. Her lip gloss? Paige's stomach sank into a new level of embarrassment.

She dug in her purse for a tissue and rushed to blot at the smudge. "I wrecked your shirt."

"It's not wrecked, Paige."

She had to hold on to his collar to help her blot better, but it didn't seem like she was getting it out of the fabric. "I'm probably making it worse."

He took light hold of her hands, as if to tell her she didn't need to keep working at the stain. But her hands were in his, close to his throat, where his pulse visibly beat just inches from her touch. "It'll wash."

Oh, how she didn't want to, but she couldn't lift her eyes from that beat of his pulse.

A light rap on the office door made her jump back. A tall woman with red hair glanced between them, and maybe Paige was seeing things, but it sure seemed like the woman's gaze fixed on the peach splotch on Kellan's collar. "I'm interrupting."

"Nope." Kellan stepped away, leaving a wide berth between himself and Paige. "Jane, meet Paige."

"We've met. You were buying books on knights and the gold rush for your kids. Did they like them?"

"They were thoroughly engaged, yes. All two dozen of them."

Had Paige heard right? "Dozen?"

Kellan chuckled. "Jane is the director of Little Lambs, the preschool on Poplar Street. Jane, Paige is studying to be a preschool teacher. She only has two courses left."

Jane's back straightened. "No kidding?"

"I can't wait." And with these online courses, she'd be one step closer.

"Then this might interest you." Jane handed over a daffodil-yellow flyer. "Those two dozen kids are in our summer program, and Monday kicks off Reading Week. Adults from the community, from TV reporters to our local independent bookstore guy here, come read to the kids. We have a few holes to fill in the schedule. Want to participate?"

What a wonderful idea. "I'd love to."

"Excellent. Are you free on Tuesday?" She

checked her phone calendar. "I roped Kellan into reading to the four-year-olds at ten, but we don't have anyone for the three-year-olds then."

"As long as it's okay with my boss that I leave work." She glanced at Kellan.

"Of course." He grinned. "We can carpool while Mickey covers the store."

Jane typed into her phone. "The kids will be so glad to see you guys. I'll have books for you to read, and Kellan, practice your quacking."

"I do not quack. Never learned," he deadpanned.

"Just open your mouth like this." Pressing the butt of her palms together like a hinge, Paige opened her hands so they made a V shape. "There's your duck bill."

"I'll leave you two to practice." Jane waved and slipped out.

Kellan grinned at Paige. "You can't wait to be around the kids, can you?"

"Nope, I can't." The realization didn't make her wistful. It reinforced where she was meant to be, working with little ones. "I'll have to wear my sparkly shoes."

His brows rose. "Do they give you super preschool powers or something?"

"You'll see." She rubbed her hands together with glee. "And you might even be a little envious."

* * *

Tuesday morning Kellan was not so much jealous of Paige's sparkly shoes as he was in awe of them. And her. The moment he and Paige arrived at Little Lambs Preschool and entered the three-year-old classroom, Paige and her shoes were surrounded.

"I like your shoes," two little girls said at once.

"Look at mine." A boy stomped his foot. The sole lit up, flashing red.

"See mine, too." This second boy's didn't light up, but they were covered with super-heroes.

Kellan responded, but there was something different, something heartfelt, in the way Paige affirmed each child with an "ooh, yes," or "I like those so much," something to make the students know she heard and acknowledged them. The teacher, the salt-and-pepper-haired Miss Alma, clearly didn't mind, since she joined in the discussion.

So did Kellan, but no one told him they liked his favorite pair of brown chukka boots.

"All right, everyone." Miss Alma clapped her hands. "Miss Paige will be reading a story to us. Sit down, criss-cross applesauce, on the rug. And I think they're ready for you now in the four-year-old room, Mr. Kellan."

Sure enough, Jane waited in the threshold, smiling at him. "The four-year-olds are finished with their snack break. Sorry to keep you waiting."

"Not at all." He enjoyed watching Paige in her element, which she clearly was. As he made his way out, he watched her take a seat in the adult-sized folding chair on the far side of the brightly hued rug. A girl with dark braids snaked out her hand to touch Paige's glittery shoes. She winked at the girl.

She opened the book with dramatic slowness and began to read the familiar Dr. Seuss story.

He could watch her all day, but he had a book to read, himself. "I don't *really* have to quack, do I, Jane?"

"Quack, chirp, caw, hoot, bock and cheep. It's a bird book." She opened the door to the four-year-old classroom. "Enjoy."

What had Paige said about making his hands into a beak? His mind went blank.

Wing it, Lambert. He imagined Paige's laughing face. *Pun intended.*

Paige read two Dr. Seuss books, but the time was over far too soon.

"Will you come back?" A boy tugged the hem of her denim jacket.

"I hope so."

"Let's thank Miss Paige," Miss Alma said, leading the children in applause.

How had Kellan done with the four-year-olds? If he wasn't accustomed to being around small kids, it could be unnerving. They tended to whisper amongst themselves, ask questions at inopportune moments—sometimes nosy questions—or have difficulty keeping their hands to themselves. That was part of what preschool was all about, though. Learning how to behave in a classroom.

And she loved every messy second of it.

But the kids had an art project now, so Paige bid the kids goodbye and met Jane in the hall. "Thanks so much for inviting me. That was wonderful."

"The kids love it when visitors read to them, but it's clear you have a knack."

"I love preschoolers. They're so guileless and curious and honest."

Unlike many adults, namely Peanut's dad. But that was not a thought worth dwelling on, here of all places. She glanced around the hallway, its walls lined with art projects and posters advertising summer gymnastics classes and nutrition programs. "Is Kellan still reading?"

Jane nodded. "Want to listen in? The door's open."

Boy, did she. As Jane excused herself to respond to an email, Paige leaned into the door-jamb of the four-year-old classroom, where the kids circled Kellan's chair. The story was about a bunch of birds—ah, yes, Jane had mentioned he'd need to quack—and Kellan made a noble effort at a deep, hearty quack. It sounded like the honking horn of an old timey car.

The kids cracked up.

Those belly laughs were like balm to the aching places in her heart, making her yearn to return to the classroom.

She'd get there. She'd registered for her education classes and ordered her textbooks online through Open Book's website, using her employee discount. Once again, she thanked God for the chance to take the classes online, and for Kellan's idea to try that particular college. Excitement coursed through her.

At once, her mother's voice had intruded into her thoughts, her imaginary tone as tart as raw rhubarb. *Why didn't you look into online courses yourself? Does Kellan have to help you with everything these days?*

Paige couldn't stop arguing with the imaginary mom in her head. She wasn't dependent on Kellan or anyone. She earned her wages, she paid her rent and bills and she'd taken measures so she and Peanut would be okay financially after the birth.

But to fully take charge of her future, she had to come to Widow's Peak Creek and wait for God's leading—the urge had been so strong to come here, she didn't fight it.

It meant swallowing her pride and asking Kellan for help. Her mom would say she was acting like a charity case, and she wouldn't understand that Kellan offered her assistance out of Christian compassion. Maybe pity, too, because he felt bad for her. He'd clearly felt sorry for her when Drew died, since he'd told her he'd help her if she needed it.

But instead of making her feel ashamed, Kellan had made her feel cared for. Normal, even, like everyone needed help sometimes.

She wanted to be that way if someone ever came to her, needing help. Not like the imaginary voice of her mom in her head, scolding and chiding.

A shriek of laughter pierced her thoughts. Coming back to the present, she focused on Kellan and the kids. He'd finished his story and high-fived a boy, the sound of their hands making a loud smack.

"Me next." A second boy jumped in front of Kellan like he was on an invisible pogo stick.

They high-fived, and next thing Paige knew, Kellan was high-fiving everyone. Up high. Down low. And too slow.

"Wing five," the first boy demanded. "Like a bird."

Kellan obliged, bending his arm like a wing and tapping the boy's elbow. Kellan exchanged the funny greeting with everyone, even though he had to bend at the knees to tap elbows with the smallest of the kids, a girl in a red sundress who couldn't hide a shy smile. Once their elbows touched, she giggled.

Did a "wing five" even exist before this? Should it be called a "high wing" instead? Whatever it was, his audience of four-year-olds thought it was hilarious.

He was so good with them. Kellan was an attractive guy already, sure, but there was something about a man with a child that made her heart expand three sizes.

Kellan looked up, catching Paige's gaze. Oh, no, did her stupid attraction show on her face? At her flush, he grinned even wider.

She spun to study the teacher's choice of decor in the reading corner. Or at least pretend to. She needed to put a stop to whatever was going on with her, before she developed feelings toward Kellan beyond those of regular old friendship.

It was one thing to need his help. But it was an entirely different thing altogether to need him.

Chapter Eight

Paige recovered her composure by the time Kellan met her in the hallway, determining to keep things light between them. Grinning, she flapped her arms like she was doing the chicken dance.

"Well-done, bird man. You should read that book for Toddler Story Time tomorrow."

"I think I have an accounting appointment then," he teased. "Hey, Jane."

The preschool director waited down the hall, palms up in a gesture of gratitude. "Thanks so much for coming, you two. You helped make Reading Week special."

Paige didn't need to think twice. "Our pleasure."

"Do you mind if I post your visit on social media? It's not bad publicity for Open Book." Jane waggled her eyebrows at Kellan.

"I don't mind. Maybe it will inspire others to read to their own kids."

"It could also show how involved you are in the community. We here at Little Lambs really appreciate Open Book. Speaking of which, Kel, you and I should get together soon to discuss September's book drive."

"Kel?" Paige didn't mean to blurt it out. She wanted to cover her mouth with her hands.

"It's easier to yell one syllable when we're cycling than to yell two, I guess." Jane chuckled.

They cycled together? Why did that bother Paige? Kellan's friends, male or female, were none of her business.

Kellan snapped his fingers. "That reminds me, the Raven Grade ride is coming up. Have you been training?"

"Of course I have, but you're changing the subject off your philanthropic endeavors." Jane turned to Paige. "Did you know Open Book donates hundreds of dollars' worth of books to Little Lambs each year? Kellan never lets us advertise it, either."

Paige didn't know much about business-type stuff, but it seemed an easy way to advertise. "Why not?"

He shrugged. "The kids are special."

Jane rolled her eyes. "Agreed, but no more

special than the other groups you team up with for book drives. Anyway, I'll let you get going." Jane pushed open the lobby's double doors for them. "Thanks again."

Paige led the way down the sidewalk away from Little Lambs, the heels of her glittery Mary Janes clacking against the sidewalk. She would *not* ask about Jane and the cycling thing. No matter how curious she was.

"Thanks for agreeing to walk instead of drive." They ambled down the sidewalk, taking a different path than the way they'd come.

"Too nice a day not to, and the exercise will do us both good." And Peanut, of course.

"So you had fun?" Kellan pushed aside a low-hanging branch of a flowering pear tree planted close to the sidewalk so it wouldn't smack her in the head.

She ducked, anyway, smiling up at him. "I loved every second. Even the smells."

"The smells?"

"White glue, hand sanitizer, Play-Doh and Cheerios." Every classroom she'd ever been in smelled like those things.

"I didn't notice. Maybe my nose is broken."

"Nah, you're just not attuned to the finer points of preschool life," she teased. They came to the corner and were about to cross Poplar Street when she realized where they were. "We're close to Creekside." The complex of buildings where Aunt Trudie lived was a short walk away.

Kellan tipped his head in a southerly direction. "Want to stop in for a visit?"

"Not now. Aunt Trudie is expecting me tomorrow after work. They're having some sort of lawn game event."

"Oh, yeah, Gran invited me. What do you suppose they mean by lawn games?" His lips twitched. "Rugby is a lawn game, isn't it?"

"Um, I was thinking horseshoes or croquet, but rugby is far more plausible in the context of games to play at a retirement village," she said in serious but teasing tone.

"I haven't played croquet since the last time I played rugby. Which was never. So either way, I'm losing tomorrow."

"So am I." Then she read the black-and-white sign hanging over an enclosed patio of green umbrella-shaded café tables. And gasped. "Mickey told me about this café. She said it has the most amazing mint lemonade. Mind if we stop?"

"It sounded like you gasped there for a second. I thought something was wrong." He glanced at her side, like he thought she might be in pain again.

"Something *is* wrong. I'm thirsty for that

lemonade. And come to think of it, I'm ravenous."

Kellan glanced at his smart watch. "Let's get mint lemonade and lunch, then. I'm hungry, too. Quacking took a lot out of me." He rubbed his stomach in an exaggerated display that told her he wasn't the least bit upset with his quacking abilities.

They sat at one of the café tables. "I thought you were quite convincing as a duck."

"I doubt that, but I don't think the preschoolers will hold it against me forever." Kellan pulled two laminated menus from between the umbrella stand and the napkin dispenser, handing one to her.

"I think you're right. They like attention and to know someone cares, just like the rest of us." She perused the menu. She wasn't usually a big fan of French dips, but for some reason, the idea of the beef, au jus and side of horseradish dipping sauce sounded so amazing right now that her stomach cramped. Peanut must *really* want a French dip.

Kellan set aside his menu. "It was a blast, for sure, but I wondered if it was hard for you, too. Because you're working in a bookstore and not a preschool."

"I am happy to be working in a bookstore, Kellan," she said with all honesty. "My motto is *there's a blue sky behind those dark clouds.* One of these days I will be working in a pre-school. That's part of my blue sky."

She'd also be a mom by then, though, and she hadn't the foggiest notion as to where God was leading. Kellan had said trusting Him could be a day-by-day decision, and she was doing her best. The destination God had in mind was worth waiting for, even if right now she couldn't see one step in front of her.

The server approached then, taking their order of two French dips—his with fries, hers with fresh fruit—and mint lemonades. Once they were alone again, Kellan tugged a few napkins out of the dispenser. "Ready for your online courses? They start soon, don't they?"

A zip that had nothing to do with hunger raced through her stomach. "I'm so excited. It looks like the lectures are prerecorded, so we view them at our own pace. I can do it all during evenings and my days off. Don't worry about me missing work time."

"I'm not worried about that at all. I know you've got this." He looked up as the server brought their lemonades. "Ah, thanks."

Paige took a sip of the minty drink. "It tastes so good." Tart things were more and more delicious these days. Peanut seemed to agree, rolling from one side of Paige's belly to the other.

Peanut's gymnastics also reminded her how blessed she was to be here in this moment, with a job, preparing for classes, and it was in large part due to Kellan. Just because the imaginary mom in her head thought the concept to be terrible didn't mean Paige shouldn't thank him. "You know I'm so grateful to you for everything you've done, right? So grateful, I'm going to order every book I ever read in the future from Open Book's website."

He didn't laugh like she'd hoped. Instead, his brow crinkled. "I'll never ask anything of you, Paige, except to take care of yourself and Peanut. And maybe, if you ever think of it, pray for me."

"Sure." About both his requests, but the second one set off a warning signal. So did the strange, blank look on his face. "Is something up?"

"Nothing new."

His expression vanished, replaced by a relieved smile at the arrival of their French dips.

She wasn't fooled. Something was causing Kellan pain. He didn't have to share it with her, but Paige wished he would.

It would be nice to ease one of his burdens for a change.

The next afternoon Kellan stood in the bocce court carved into the yard behind Creekside Retirement Village, weighing a ball in his hand. Two pounds, maybe? Heavy enough to give it some force when tossed, but light enough to allow for a soft touch.

"I think we can take them, Gran."

Her bony fingers patted his forearm. "I think *you* can take them, honey. You and Paige team up against Ralph and Stu here."

"And we're pretty good," retorted one of the older fellows nearby as he hooked his thumbs through his bright blue suspenders.

Paige's eyes widened. "I'm sorry, Eileen, but I'm teamed with Aunt Trudie."

Trudie glanced at Gran and Marigold, who'd come along today. Kellan had heard from Paige that the three of them were part of a knitting group, but he hadn't realized they were as close as they were. At least, they seemed to be close, the way they'd been whispering or exchanging meaningful looks since Kellan and Paige arrived. "Actually, Paige, Eileen, Marigold and I prefer to play horseshoes."

Then why hadn't they led them to the horseshoes instead of taking them straight to the bocce court? Kellan dropped the bocce ball. "Sure. Let's go. I'll even play croquet, if you want."

Paige's smile warmed him. Clearly, she

remembered their little joke from yesterday about croquet and rugby.

"Nonsense." Gran's touch on his back felt like a push into the bocce court. "Bocce needs even numbers, so you two play with Stu and Ralph."

Paige's brows lifted. "I'm happy to sit out—"

"Oh, we'd never ask that of you, dear Paige." Marigold's wave was almost like a shoo. "Have fun and we'll meet up soon."

"Can we get the show on the road now?" The man in the blue suspenders picked up the small, white *pallino* ball from the grass. "Stu here's waited all day for this."

So Mr. Blue Suspenders was Ralph, and the other fellow in the yellow dress shirt and newsboy cap was Stu. Stu gestured at the packed-dirt court. "Ready?"

"We're ready." Paige smiled at the older gentlemen. Then she leaned into Kellan, carrying with her the heady scent of flowers and fruit. "That was weird of our relatives, right?" she murmured. "Forcing us to play bocce?"

"Most definitely weird." He watched Ralph roll his shoulders. "You know how to play?"

"I think we each get two bocce balls and we're aiming to hit the white ball. Or at least be closer to it than Ralph or Stu. I should warn you, though, the only way I've ever played was a plastic set with preschoolers. Are you any good at this?"

"Let's just say the last time I played, it was also with a plastic set."

She looked into his eyes. "They're going to beat us, Lambert."

"Yup."

Ralph tossed the first of his two bocce balls at the *pallino*. The larger ball didn't strike it, but it had come close.

"Nice job, Ralph," Paige called. "Do you play often?"

"Less talkin', more playin', missy."

Clearly, this was serious business for Ralph. Kellan bit back a smile as Paige rolled her first ball like a bowling ball toward the *pallino*. It fell a yard short.

While Stu took his first turn of the round, Kellan considered his options. He could try to strike the *pallino*, or he could try to hit Paige's ball, moving it closer. Or, if he was really going to play this game with some strategy, he'd aim for Ralph's ball and try to knock it farther away from the *pallino*.

Stu's ball struck the *pallino* with a soft *clonk*. An enviable position.

"Come on, Kellan," Paige cheered.

Kellan stepped into place and breathed deeply of the lavender and other shrubs bordering the court. Kellan was grateful to be out in the fresh air, rather than inside, where it probably smelled like disinfectant that would trigger a repeat of his last visit here.

God, I hope someday You'll see fit to free me from associating that smell with the night of Drew's death.

But if not? It was up to God. He had to trust that.

He tossed the ball.

"Pretty good." Paige clapped.

"Humph." Ralph glared at the ball, an inch away from Stu's.

Win or lose, Kellan didn't care. Today's event was all about fun and spending time with others, although he'd expected to spend time with Gran.

Speaking of Gran, she, Trudie and Marigold stood near the empty horseshoe pit across the yard, not playing, but chattering and shooting darting glances at the bocce court. Paige turned to follow his gaze, then shot a question at Kellan with her eyes.

"You're up, missy," Ralph barked. "Pay attention, now."

"Yes, sir." Paige tossed her ball, knocking her first one closer and returning to Kellan's side. "Have you noticed our ladies are staring at us?"

"Yup." Kellan tossed his ball once Stu finished. His ball grazed Ralph's but not enough to win the round. "Point to you, fellas."

"Ten more to go." Stu pumped his fist.

"You know what they're doing, don't you?" Kellan scooped up Paige's bocce balls and handed them to her for the next round's play.

"I am so embarrassed to say it aloud, but it's obvious they're trying to get us together. I'm sorry, Kellan."

"You have nothing to be embarrassed about. They're doing it to be sweet, but they don't have all the facts. Like how neither of us is exactly open to a relationship right now."

"I guess I should have told Aunt Trudie about my decision to raise the baby alone, yeah." She tossed her ball, and it nicked the *pallino*. "I didn't know you weren't, um, open, though. You're not dating? I thought maybe you and Jane. Because you cycle together."

"Jane?" Stu took his turn fast, and Kellan had to toss his ball before he could respond, since clearly Stu and Ralph preferred to play than chat. "We're both in a cycling club. We ride and have occasional meetings at The World Outside store. But no. Never even crossed my radar. I don't date. Not for a while now." Probably not ever. "I've made that clear to my mom, but maybe I need to put a bug in Gran's ear, too."

"Why don't you date?" Paige asked. Then she blanched. "Sorry. None of my business."

He couldn't tell her the truth, so he shrugged. "I just think it's my lot."

"Should we confront them now?" Paige's question was rushed as she hurried to toss her ball. When she returned, she stared at their relatives and neighbor.

Confrontation might not do any good. Paige had her reasons for staying single, but she was open about them. Kellan, however, would have to explain things he didn't want to discuss. Gran and Marigold knew him well, but they weren't among the few people who knew what had happened in Afghanistan. That Kellan was responsible for Drew's death.

How could he live a happy, full life with a wife and kids when he'd made a mistake that cost Drew his life?

This wasn't the time or place to dwell on it, though. Instead, he smiled at Paige. "I think we should ignore them and have fun."

"I do, too."

Kellan tipped his head at Stu and Ralph. "We can't let them take us down in a clean sweep."

"No way. Let's put up a fight."

And they did, playing for best two out of three games, but they lost. It was one of the most enjoyable losses of Kellan's memory. And when they finished, he kissed Gran's cheek and he and Paige left, letting the older ladies wonder if their little matchmaking plan would bear any fruit.

It wouldn't, of course, but he went to sleep that night reliving the sounds of Paige's laughter and the balls plunking on the hard dirt court, watching the way the breeze captured tendrils of her hair and brushed them across her cheeks.

He didn't stay asleep, though. He jolted awake in the darkness, drenched in sweat, gasping for breath, the scar on his thigh prickling with remembered pain. In his sleep, he'd been back in Afghanistan, reliving Drew's death.

But Paige appeared in the dream, staring at Kellan with grief-stricken eyes. *You did this?*

Kellan wiped his damp brow, slowly coming out of the nightmare. He sucked in a deep breath, held it for a count of four and exhaled slowly, praying all the while for peace. Then something whimpered near his knee. Jet?

In the darkness, Kellan reached for the dog, surprised to find Gladys alongside Jet, beside him atop the covers. A light pressure descended on the far side of the bed—Frank? His left hand met the cat's silky back.

The animals didn't usually congregate together like this with him on the bed. Kellan must have cried out or thrashed in his sleep and they'd come to investigate.

Kellan stroked their fur and felt his pulse slow. *Thank you for these animals, God.*

"It's all right now, guys."

Except that it wasn't. That dream showed him something had shifted inside him. He wasn't just grieving over Drew's death anymore, or suffering guilt over his part in it. Now, on top of it, he feared Paige would learn the truth.

And she'd hate him for it, which had become an intolerable thing to bear.

Chapter Nine

"How's the coffee, Herb?" Saturday morning as Paige restocked the magazine shelf, she couldn't help but notice Herb's paper cup was still full of the dark brew. In her almost two weeks working at Open Book, she hadn't once seen Herb limit himself to a few sips.

Herb's lips twisted like he'd nibbled lemon. "Did you make it?"

This was going to be the longest conversation they'd had yet, and Paige felt like clapping. "No, I didn't. Kellan usually does."

"I don't think so." Herb frowned at it. "It's chewy."

"Oh, we can't have that. May I?" Paige took the cup. Sure enough, grounds clung to the sides. "I suspect something got clogged in the machine. I'll take care of it right away."

She cradled the pump dispenser in her arm like a full grocery bag.

"You okay to be carrying anything?" His gruff voice held her back. "What about your young'un?"

Her heart almost exploded at this uncharacteristic fountain of words from Herb. "The baby's fine. So fine that he or she woke me up twice in the night kicking." She fisted a hand on her hip for effect.

"Don't be upset about the kicking." He returned his focus on the travel magazine on his lap. "Used to keep my wife up, too. I was in the army, stationed in Germany, no family near us. And she'd wake me up so I could feel it, but I'd get irritated because I had to work in the mornings. Turns out, though, my late wife and I never got to see our young'uns' faces. Well, not me, anyway. My wife can see 'em now that she's gone on to glory."

Paige's heart dropped to her stomach. "Oh, Herb."

"Paige?" Kellan came out from an aisle. "Everything all right? Here, let me take that."

She transferred the dispenser to him. "The coffee's full of grounds."

"It's chewy," Herb added.

"Sorry about that. I'll brew a new pot right away." Kellan carried the dispenser to the kitchen, and Paige followed after him to dump out the cup.

"What a mess." Grounds smeared the brewer like clumps of mud.

Kellan grabbed a rag. "Mickey must not have noticed when she brewed the coffee."

"You don't sound angry." Every boss Paige had ever had would be irritated, to say the least. He didn't even mutter under his breath.

"Getting angry won't help anything."

"I'll try to remember that the next time I make a mistake. I'm pretty good at beating myself up over things."

His smile faded as he measured fresh grounds into the brewer. "You're not alone, but in the grand scheme of things, this isn't that big of a mistake."

This wasn't the first time his expression turned blank like this. It had happened before, at times she couldn't pinpoint, but definitely at the café when he asked her to pray for him. He didn't specify what needed prayer in particular, but she knew something was off, then and now. She couldn't be imagining the lack of emotion in his eyes. Or the squared set of his shoulders.

Before she could ask what was wrong, he pushed the button to start a fresh pot of coffee. "There, Herb will have a new cup in no time."

In other words, Kellan did not wish to discuss anything deeper than coffee. Fine. She'd go along with it. For now.

"Does Herb ever buy anything?" As the rich aroma of coffee filled the kitchenette, she rinsed out the coffee-stained rags in the sink.

"Not when I'm working register." A diplomatic answer if she'd ever heard one. "Not that I expect him to buy anything. He comes to look at magazines and hang out."

"I think it has less to do with the coffee and magazines and more with being alone. He and his late wife never had any babies that lived." Her hand went to her tummy in an instinctive gesture.

His gaze followed her hand before he looked her in the eye. "I had no idea. That's awful."

"It's a good reminder that all of us have some trouble and sadness in our pasts. You never know."

"No, you don't." There was Kellan's weird expression again.

An alarm of warning went off in Paige's head. She'd experienced this sensation so many times before, mainly in her relationships with men—not that she'd had more than a few—and she'd ignored the red flags each time.

One thing her time with Aidan had taught her, though, was her instincts shouldn't be ignored. God had given her a brain, and this time she was going to use it. "What's wrong, Kellan?"

He looked at her, almost startled. "What?"

"Is something—"

"Kellan, can you come out? Don's here." Hand on the threshold, Mickey peered into the kitchenette. Then her gaze caught on the trash can full of grounds. "I did that?"

"Easy fix." Kellan slipped past her out of the kitchenette. Mickey followed after him, apologizing. Paige could hear his reassurances as they returned to the store.

She watched the last of the coffee drip into the pot and contemplated Kellan's rare moments of—what were they? Melancholy? Distance? Whatever bothered him wasn't any of her business, but she couldn't help but want to help him.

"Paige?" Kellan's mom lingered in the doorway.

"Hi, Belinda. Want a cup? It's just about ready." The last few dribbles landed in the pot.

"I'd love some, thanks."

Paige poured two cups, one for Belinda, another for Herb, before filling the pump dispenser. "There's milk in the fridge if you like."

"This is perfect." Belinda set down the cup without taking a sip. "I'm glad for a moment alone with you. Sounds like you and Kellan had fun playing bocce at Creekside the other day."

Gossip traveled faster than the water flowed in the creek. "We did."

"Kellan doesn't have enough fun, if you ask me. No time for a social life."

"He told me he attends a Wednesday morning Bible study with other guys at Del's Café. The pastor attends, too. They seem like good friends to me."

"You're friends with him, too, I take it."

Paige's ears grew hot. "Yes."

Belinda's well-plucked brows pulled together. "Then maybe you can convince him to join the veterans' group over in Pinehurst. Maybe among his peers, he'll be able to talk through his PTSD."

Paige's throat tightened. "Kellan has PTSD?"

"He hides it well, but he isn't the same as he was before his military service. He has these dark moments. Surely, you've noticed it."

Was that what she'd perceived? Was he hiding post-traumatic stress?

He shouldn't be dealing with it alone.

He shouldn't be dealing with it at all, poor man.

"I'm so sorry. How can I support him?"

"Like I said, he could benefit from that group." Belinda sipped her coffee. "Certain things set him off. Not that he'll talk to me about it, but I have my suspicions. Has he mentioned anything to you about it?"

"Nothing."

"Have you noticed anything, then? Does he withdraw at the mention of particular subjects? Like perhaps his time in the service? Or your brother?"

The blood in Paige's ears drained to her toes. The loss of Drew had been horrible for her and her mom, but they hadn't been there when it happened. Unlike Kellan.

It took her a moment to find the ability to speak. "I'll be more watchful. Now, if you'll pardon me a moment, I need to deliver this cup to Herb."

"Of course, Paige."

Herb gratefully—and silently—accepted the cup. He blew on the contents and slurped, giving her a thumbs-up. He must be all talked out for the day.

But she wasn't. Not with Kellan, anyway. At the end of her shift, a half hour after his mom and Don had gone, she found him in the office. He shut the filing cabinet and smiled at her. "Heading out?"

"Almost." She licked her lips. "Can I ask you something?"

"Of course."

"Is my being here a problem for you?"

He flinched. "What? Why do you ask that?"

"Because of something your mom said. I'm worried my presence is dredging up memories of the night Drew died. Am I causing you difficulties? Because if I am, I'll quit Open Book. Right now."

Kellan's scalp felt scorched by a sudden heat. It didn't take a mathematical whiz to add two and two—his mom had been in the store and now Paige was asking him about his emotional state. "My mom told you she thinks I have PTSD?"

"She did, and if I'm making it worse, I'll go."

"You are not causing me any difficulties." Not like that, anyway. He cared for her, and yes, he was attracted to her, but he'd determined not to allow any feelings to grow.

Nevertheless, now that he'd grown closer to her, he feared her leaving his life completely once she learned the truth.

If she learned the truth.

But was she a contributing factor to his stress? No.

More important, though, was that regardless of his struggles, he was honor bound to support Paige however he could. He owed Drew that and more, so he met her uncertain gaze. "I don't want you to quit Open Book unless you want to, Paige. When you come to a decision about your future, or have a better opportunity, or even because you don't like working here. But certainly not because of some bee in my mom's bonnet."

Paige's dark lashes fanned her cheeks as she stared down at her black leather booties. "Do I remind you of Drew, though? Because if I do, or being around me triggers you, that has to hurt."

"Of course you remind me of him. But that doesn't mean—"

He broke off as a shadow passed outside the office door. Mickey? A customer using the restroom? Regardless of who it was, they couldn't have this talk here. Nor could he let this wait until tonight. "Do you have a minute to take the recycling out with me?"

"Sure."

He grabbed the half-full wire wastebasket by the filing cabinet and carried it out the back door, into an alley just wide enough for trash trucks to drive through. Once out in the bright June sunlight, it took two seconds to toss the cardboard and wastepaper into the blue recycling dumpster. Both of them knew, though, that coming out here had nothing to do with getting rid of recyclables.

God, give me words. Ones that will protect her from pain.

He joined her at the back door, in the narrow shade of the decorative overhang above their heads. "You do remind me of Drew, but that isn't a bad thing. He was more than a member of my squad. He was my best friend. I miss him. Don't I remind you of Drew, too? Because he's how we met?"

He'd been on leave for Thanksgiving the year before Drew died. Kellan's mom and sister were on some holiday cruise, so he'd gone home with Drew to Sacramento, not so far from where he'd grown up. He'd enjoyed an afternoon of watching football with the Faradays, followed by a festive turkey dinner.

Paige had been bubbly and light and welcoming.

Over five years had passed, but she was still as light and lovely. Although right now her brow creased. "I see your point. We have him in common."

"Exactly." He rubbed his aching forehead. "My mom means well, but she was out of line, saying that you trigger me. She's wrong, and I'm sorry she said that."

"She didn't precisely say I'm a *trigger*. I inferred it. And she wasn't blaming me for anything. More like she was bringing her concerns to my attention in the hopes I would encourage you to talk to someone." Paige leaned against the brick store wall, arms folded across her chest. "She said something about the veterans' group in Pinehurst."

"They're a great group of people. But the group is for PTSD—a response to trauma, as natural as bleeding from a cut, nothing of which to be ashamed. But while I have a few common symptoms, I don't tick enough boxes, according to the army counselor I spoke to. He was confident that I do not have PTSD."

The counselor was also confident that Kellan suffered from survivor's guilt and resulting anxiety. He suggested Kellan could benefit from a group therapy session.

Kellan resisted, though. For one thing, he had no desire to intrude on a group of people who'd been through so much more than he had, suffering from something Kellan wasn't diagnosed with.

But the other reason ached like his gunshot wound on a winter night. He'd tried sharing his experience and subsequent feelings right after the incident, and it hadn't gone well. Everyone, from his superiors to his friends, listened long enough to tell him Drew's death wasn't his fault. But they always looked away, giving the impression they were lying.

Well, all except for his pastor, Benton.

But everyone else? Why would things go better in a group therapy session? Kellan couldn't go through that anymore. Nope, he was on his own, and God had given him ways to deal with his anguish. Including this opportunity to repay Drew. Helping Paige.

She looked at him now with a softer expression, but her eyes were still wary. "I'm glad you talked to someone, but I'm sorry for what you went through, all at the same time."

"Life is messy. What was it you said earlier, we all have stuff in our pasts? Well, Afghanistan is a big thing in mine. But despite that, I don't want to forget Drew. Not ever."

Not the end, or the good times, either. And there had been plenty of those.

"Me, neither. But I don't want to cause anyone trouble. And lately, it seems like that's all I do." Her hand went to her rounded stomach.

His pulse ratcheted. "Is Peanut okay?"

"Oh, yeah. Fine." She laughed. "All I meant is, I made some choices that led me here. I'm a lot of trouble. I'm not self-sufficient yet. I don't have a plan yet."

"That doesn't make you trouble, Paige."

"It makes me a burden."

"That's not true." He folded his arms, just like she did. "If you don't mind me turning this into an employee review, here? You're a bright addition to Open Book. All of your ideas for revamping the kids' section? They're great. Already a handful of parents told me they're more comfortable now that we've increased the space for Toddler Story Time. It's going to be our loss when you move on from Widow's Peak Creek to pursue your goals."

The thought of her being a preschool teacher at last warmed him to the core. The only problem with it was it meant she'd leave.

Her smile spread from self-deprecating to the one she wore when she was pleased, like when she engaged with preschoolers at Little Lambs. "That's really sweet of you, Kellan. Thank you."

"It's the truth."

"Is it okay if I hug my boss? My friend?" She reached out with one arm for a half hug.

"Sure." It started awkward, his arm stiff with shock at having her so close to him.

Then she turned into him slightly and sighed, her warm breath fanning his skin.

"Other than Aunt Trudie, I haven't had a hug in a while."

"Me, neither." Something relaxed in their embrace and he rested his cheek atop her head.

He didn't want to leave this alley, despite the dumpsters and empty milk crates and cardboard boxes. He wanted—

He wanted to hold on to Paige with both arms. Hold her close. It was time he admitted it to himself.

Back on that night that she gave him the banana bread, he determined not to form an emotional connection to her. He'd been an idiot, though, because it had already been too late for that.

He couldn't ignore it now, but that didn't mean he would do anything about it. His feelings had to still be small enough to control. He would channel those feelings into helping Paige. Supporting her in a tough time. Being a friend while she was in Widow's Peak Creek.

Nevertheless, it was difficult not to think about how easy it would be to tip his head and kiss her vibrant hair, so soft against his cheek.

She let out a small cry.

He let go, but she blinked as if confused as she stared up at him. "What was that sound?"

"It wasn't you?"

"No."

A second high-pitched whimper pierced the air. Definitely not Paige.

The alley was empty, devoid of any workers from the other businesses on the west side of Main Street. To his left, no one passed on Creek Street. They were utterly alone. Well, almost.

He dropped to his haunches and peered beneath the large recycling dumpster. Sure enough, there it was, a small thing staring at him from the dim.

He patted his leg. "Come on out."

"What is it?" Paige crouched at his shoulder.

"A puppy." Gently, slowly, he offered his fingers for sniffing. After a few hesitant back-and-forth attempts, the dog wriggled closer and its damp, black button of a nose investigated his hand. "Bright blue eyes, too. Come on out, little one."

At last, the pup allowed him to scoop it into his arms. "There we are. You're safe."

Oohing, Paige rubbed the puppy's head, dirty though it was. "No collar. I wonder who it belongs to."

"I've never seen her before." She was a cutie, though. Beneath the mud flecks, she was speckled brown and black, except for gold cheeks and a white muzzle and front legs. She cuddled into his chest, small even for a puppy, so she probably wouldn't get to be as big as either Jet or Gladys. She was also lean, her tummy concave against his hand. "You need food and water, don't you?"

"You poor little thing. We don't have puppy chow but the water, we can manage. I'll get a bowl from the break room."

"And after that, we'll call the vet to get you checked out before they close for the day." Kellan lifted the puppy so he could look her in her striking blue eyes.

She didn't know it, but she was a gift of God, sent at just the right time. Close as he'd been to kissing Paige, this pup had saved him from making a huge mistake.

Chapter Ten

A few hours later Paige knocked on Kellan's front door, her fist rapping hard and fast on the gray painted wood. He'd promised to keep her updated on the puppy's trip to the vet, but clearly she and Kellan had differing opinions about what updating meant. She'd expected a play-by-play. He, obviously, meant he'd let her know he was home. His text from a few seconds ago informed her of the fact and invited her over.

He hadn't said a word about dog. Nothing about the puppy's health, or if she'd been microchipped and reunited with her owner, or if she was safe. Maddening man. Paige stepped into her flip-flops and charged to his house.

He opened the door while she was still knocking. Jet and Gladys pounced on her, their wet noses on her legs, but her gaze caught on Kellan and the puppy cradled to his chest. She didn't waste her breath on a hello. "You're keeping her?"

"If no one comes forward to claim her." He didn't seem unhappy at the prospect, judging by his smile as he beckoned her inside the foyer.

After greeting Jet and Gladys with pats, Paige dropped her house key on the lacquered credenza and reached out to the puppy, letting her sniff her hand. She was damp, all traces of mud were gone and the scent of baby shampoo permeated the air. "You had a bath, little bug."

"She's so small, I could clean her off in the garage sink. Quick and easy."

Much easier than bathing Gladys and Jet, probably. The two older dogs panted at Paige's side, so she resumed rubbing them both down so they wouldn't feel neglected. She had never had multiple dogs, but surely they, like preschoolers, enjoyed getting a share of the attention. "So she wasn't microchipped?"

Kellan shook his head. "She didn't have a tattoo that some vets use to indicate a completed surgery, either. I put a notice for a found puppy on the neighborhood phone app, but I'm guessing she doesn't belong to anyone. She's so thin, I think she's been on her own awhile.

She ate a good serving of puppy food at the vet's, and she ate more after her bath."

"Where'd you come from, little bug?" Paige left the older dogs to stroke the puppy's shoulders. "Could she have run away?"

Kellan's lips twisted. "Much as I hate to say it, it's possible someone dumped her."

How could a person do that, when there were other options available? Then again, her ex-fiancé Aidan lied to her about her living situation, and then dumped her and the baby, so yeah, some people were capable of all kinds of things.

"Come on in." Kellan tipped his head, indicating they should move into the living room. A small, well-used dog bed had been added to the older dogs' cushions, and pet toys scattered around the floor. He set down the puppy, and Gladys and Jet settled down on the gray rug by the hearth to watch the pup chew a rope toy. Frank, the gray cat, perched above it all on a chair back, aware but not making a fuss over the new addition.

"The other animals seem to like her." Paige dropped onto the comfortable sofa.

"They're easygoing, that's for sure."

A knock sounded from the front door, and every set of ears—three canine, one feline—

perked up. "No clue who that could be. Just a second."

"Sure." Paige rolled a ball to the puppy, who pounced on it, gripping it with her oversize paws. From behind her, she could hear Kellan open the door, and a cheerful voice filled the house. Marigold was here.

"Oh, Paige dear, I'm sorry to intrude on you two." Marigold bit her smiling lower lip.

Ugh, was Marigold's mind still on making a match of Paige and Kellan? Marigold, Aunt Trudie and Eileen had been so obvious the other day at Creekside, forcing that game of bocce and watching them like eager-eyed chaperones in a Jane Austen novel.

Part of her didn't care what the women thought of her relationship with Kellan, as long as she and Kellan were on the same page. Which they were. The Friend Page.

But the other part of her didn't want Marigold to misinterpret Paige's presence here, so she stood up. "No intrusion. I came to see the puppy."

"Me, too. Kellan texted me about her." Marigold greeted the other pets first before bending down to let the puppy sniff her hand. "What a darling. She's an interesting mix of breeds, isn't she?"

Kellan gestured that Marigold should take a

seat. "The vet thinks she's part corgi, accounting for her size and shape, but her coloring makes us wonder if she's also part Australian shepherd. So I'm thinking of calling her Sydney."

Ah, for Sydney, Australia. Paige approved. "I think the name fits her well."

"So you're keeping her?" Marigold adjusted the nylon fabric of her turquoise skirt as she made herself comfortable on the couch.

"Unless someone claims her." Kellan crooked his thumb in the direction of the kitchen. "Do either of you want something to eat? I'm going to make a sandwich."

Marigold waved her hand. "Thanks, dear, but I've already eaten."

So had Paige, a container of leftover pasta primavera, but a sandwich sounded good. Her first trimester of pregnancy, she'd suffered morning sickness and hadn't had much of an appetite, but now, every once in a while, she was so hungry she couldn't get full. Maybe those occasions meant the baby was about to have a growth spurt. "Maybe a half sandwich?" She followed Kellan to the kitchen.

He pulled some turkey from his fridge, along with condiments and a jar of Paige's favorite brand of pickles. She glanced around the neat kitchen. "How can I help?"

"Bread's in the pantry along with some chips."

She found them easily, her stomach rumbling at the sight of the bright yellow bag of chips. She didn't need the empty calories, but they looked so good. Just a few, then. She followed Kellan's lead, assembling her half sandwich at the kitchen island beside him. "Mmm, I love these pickles."

"That's the cliché, right? Pregnant women want pickles?" The corner of his mouth lifted in a half smile.

"Pickles and ice cream is what I've heard, but ice cream doesn't sound good right now. Not like pickles, which I can't get enough of. Or these chips." For emphasis, she popped one into her mouth. Oh, so salty and good. Peanut was definitely craving potato chips. "Thanks for the food."

"Are you sure you don't want a bigger sandwich?" Glancing down at her plate, he reached across her for the mustard. A decidedly doggish cluster of short brown hairs coated his dark green shirtsleeve. She started to brush them away but stopped herself, disguising the movement by taking more chips.

She had no business touching him, even for something as innocent as whisking puppy fur from his shirt. Today's hug with him was an anomaly. One of those things to communicate

she heard and understood him and felt understood in return.

But the hug she and Kellan had shared
wasn't one of those "there-there" sort of things.
It had lingered. And even though it was a half
hug, it felt…electric. Meaningful. She'd even
thought he might turn and kiss her.

Super ridiculous thought. She'd probably
imagined the whole thing.

Except that her initial response to it was
to *want* him to kiss her. If he'd lowered his
head, she would have lifted hers and kissed
him back.

*Don't go down this road. Do not. Think
about anything other than kissing Kellan.* She
shoved a chip into her mouth.

Kellan bypassed the dining table and led
them back into the living room, where Jet
rested his sleek muzzle on Marigold's lap. She
adjusted her orange-framed glasses. "There's
a lot of love in this house, Kellan."

He sat adjacent to her. "They give so much,
don't they?"

"I meant you."

"God gave them to me, not the other way
around."

"I'm not so sure about that. You're a special
fellow, dear lad."

He shook his head and took a large bite of sandwich.

Paige nibbled hers, but what Marigold had said was true. Kellan was a unique man. He changed the subject to the visit to the veterinarian, and Paige listened with half an ear. Her focus fixed more on watching him interact with the pets and Marigold, of whom he was clearly fond. Offering her a chip. Rolling the ball to Sydney. Reminding Gladys she'd had her own dinner and this was his turkey sandwich.

It was impossible not to compare him to Aidan, or any other man she'd ever been in a relationship with. None of them was as big-hearted as Kellan, as caring or kind to people without ever wanting anything in return. He loved Marigold. He provided coffee for Herb because he had nowhere else to hang out. He did book drives for the preschool and other worthy groups, according to Jane. He took in animals. And helped Paige. Why?

Because he was kind. No other reason.

Her mind returned to their hug in the alley. The electricity of it. She'd already admitted to herself that she was attracted to him, but now she needed to accept another fact.

Her attraction to him wasn't one-sided. Maybe he hadn't thought about kissing her there in the alley, but that didn't mean she imagined the electricity of that moment. He felt something, too.

And others had seen it. It must be the reason Aunt Trudie had joined up with Marigold and Eileen to play matchmakers. It wasn't just that they thought Paige and Kellan were lonely or might make a good pair. They'd acted in response to a connection they'd observed between them.

When Paige made her decision to remain single, she'd assumed anyone she might date in the future would leave and break their hearts. Her assumption was based on experience, and the only way she knew with 100 percent certainty that she could provide a home of stability and love was to do it herself.

But what if she was involved with someone who would never abandon them? Who kept his promises and told the truth, who didn't keep secrets?

Someone like Kellan?

Stop. Stop. She'd made this decision in the clear light of reality. She could admit to being attracted to Kellan, but she couldn't let her feelings grow any more than that.

Besides, he'd straight up told her he didn't want to date. He was happy being single. So he wasn't available, anyway.

But when he scooped Sydney from the floor to nuzzle her little face, it was difficult to keep the gates of her heart shut. Especially now that she believed he felt the pull between them, too.

Lord, help me stay strong. If I unlock those gates, I'm afraid they'll burst wide open and I'll be a goner.

The next morning Kellan stood in front of his closet and stared at his ties. A blue stripe. A tasteful floral, scattered with pastel blooms. One covered with books that his mom had given him. She'd also gifted him with the tie bedecked with Christmas trees.

Any would complement the pale blue oxford dress shirt he'd donned for church this morning. Except the Christmas one, of course.

His congregation was the sort where a man could get by as easily wearing jeans as a three-piece suit, but he generally wore a dress shirt, a step up from what he wore to work at Open Book. Today was different, though, because Paige was attending church with him. The urge to dress up was strong.

"But this is not a date," he told the ties. To prove it, he'd invited Gran and Trudie along, offering to pick them up. At Gran's snort, he'd told her church isn't a date-type thing.

Even over the phone, he could tell Gran rolled her eyes.

But church was not a date. It was *church*. And he was taking a friend and their relatives who lived at Creekside. They were practically carpooling.

Kellan decided against the tie. He ensured the animals had food and water, crated Sydney with some chew toys and pulled the locked door behind him—running smack into Paige, hand raised to knock on his front door.

She looked pretty, in a yellow-and-white floral dress he'd never seen before. She also looked concerned, with her lips twisted like that.

"About church," she said. "I'm not sure I should go."

"Why not? Unless—are you sick?" Yesterday she'd seemed fine.

"No. I'm just…huge." She gestured at her midsection.

He wanted to retort that yeah, she was pregnant, but his gut warned him that wouldn't be the right thing to say. "You're not huge at all, Paige."

His diplomatic attempt didn't do a thing to soothe the worried line creasing her brow. "Well, I'm obviously having a baby, and there's nothing short of wearing a circus tent that would disguise that fact."

Why would she want to? He was way out of his depth here. Praying for guidance, he rubbed his forehead. "Are you worried about... what, particularly?"

"Up until this morning, I wasn't showing that much, but I sure am today. It's like Peanut grew overnight and I couldn't fit into the dress I planned to wear today."

That would be weird. "That's good, though, right? It means Peanut is thriving."

She sighed. "Yes, but now it's blatantly obvious that I'm pregnant. And I'm not married. I knew people would figure out I'm expecting, of course, but visiting church with you? I don't want to embarrass you. Especially if you're worried people will get the wrong impression."

So that's what this was about. "I don't care what people think, but if they do judge, they're forgetting where they are. And who they are. Church is a place full of imperfect people."

"Yeah, but my missteps are more obvious than other people's. And I worry Peanut will be judged for my mistake, now and for the rest of his or her life."

At least she was walking toward his truck now, so apparently, she was indeed going to church.

He swung her door open. "First of all, if anyone says a word to you about why you're in church as an unwed mom, Benton, the pastor, will have something to say about it. And so will I, but I might not be as kind as he will."

He made his way around the hood and climbed behind the wheel. "Second, when it comes to the rest of Peanut's life? He or she has a tremendous example of love and gentleness in you, because if you encounter any judgment, you'll handle it well because you know they're coming from a place of brokenness themselves. You're the one who reminded me that not a single person we meet is free of pain."

"When we were talking about Herb?"

"Yeah, that was it." He pulled onto the road.

"And then your mom told me about her concerns about you."

"That I have PTSD. Which I don't."

"Maybe not, but it made me think. Is something troubling you?"

His stomach sank. "What do you mean?"

"You get a look on your face sometimes, like you're in a dark place. In your head." She shifted in her seat to better face him. "I know you talked to a counselor, but if you need to talk some more, I'm happy to listen. You told me everyone needs help sometimes, right? So let me help you."

Pain sluiced through his chest like his heart was literally cracking. "That's really sweet of you, Paige, but I'm okay."

He felt her heavy stare for a few moments before she turned away, either disbelieving that he was okay or upset that he didn't want to confide in her. Or both. Great, now she thought he was a hypocrite.

Well, he was, wasn't he? Wanting her to let him help bear her burdens but shouldering his himself?

He had to, though. If he shared his secret, she'd be devastated.

Meanwhile they'd arrived at Creekside Retirement Village. Gran and Trudie waited outside for them, wearing huge smiles and their Sunday bests. Much as he felt he should say something more to Paige to smooth things over, there was no time. He exited the truck to open the rear door for the ladies.

Paige started to scramble out of the front seat—to offer the spot to one of their relatives or to get away from him, he wasn't sure—but Gran waved her off. "The back seat is perfectly roomy, thank you."

"Good morning," Trudie said in a joyful voice.

His and Paige's greetings weren't quite as cheery. In the rearview mirror, he caught the confused look exchanged by his grandma and Paige's great-aunt.

He also noticed they both held large Tupperware containers on their laps. "What do you two have there?"

"It's potluck Sunday. Don't you remember?"

Before he could answer that he did not remember that at all, Paige's hands went to her cheeks. "I don't have anything to share."

"You don't need anything." Kellan turned out of the parking lot into traffic. "You're a guest."

"A big-as-a-whale guest," she muttered.

"I'll run out after the service to pick up something for us to share."

"Nonsense. Ours are big enough to come from you two, as well." Trudie's hand snaked from the back seat to pat both of their shoulders. "Eileen baked her Texas sheet cake, and I made enough taco salad for a crowd."

"Thanks." Paige stared out the window, clearly still frustrated. What about her motto that there was a blue sky behind those dark clouds? Now would be a good time to remember that blue sky.

But he couldn't say that to her. Nor could he ask what else might be bothering her, besides being worried about others' opinions. Or delve into why she wanted him to confide in her.

God, how do I handle this? I can't come clean with her. I don't want to lie to her, either. What do You want from me right now?

Feeling this helpless was not something he was accustomed to.

Chapter Eleven

Kellan usually sat near some friends from his Wednesday morning Bible study group, but today he followed Trudie and Gran to the pew of their choosing. The opening hymn was joyful and uplifting, but the tension between him and Paige didn't ease much during the worship service. Paige sat as far from him as possible, with Trudie and Gran between them on the pew. If she wanted the other parishioners to know she and Kellan weren't an item, she was doing a great job of it.

They didn't even seem like friends.

Nevertheless, that was how he introduced her to Benton, the pastor, after the service. "Meet my friend, Paige Faraday."

"Paige, welcome." Dark-haired and fit, Benton was in his midthirties and single. Which made all the church ladies get ideas about introducing him to their daughters or nieces. But Benton was focused on tending his flock, not looking for a spouse. He shook Paige's hand and grinned. "I've heard a lot about you."

Her free hand fluttered, like it wanted to cover her rounded midsection. "You have?"

"Kellan's a good friend. He tells me you're working at Open Book."

That was about all Kellan had told him, though, other than she was Drew Faraday's sister.

Appreciative of Benton's warm welcome for Paige, Kellan clapped his shoulder. "The sermon hit me harder than usual today, Ben. You obviously put a lot of preparation into your messages."

"Indeed," Gran said. "But we'll let you finish up here so you can hurry over to the parish hall to bless the food."

"Every bachelor pastor like myself loves a good potluck. I'm not as good a cook as Kellan is. See you all in there."

"That's not true," Trudie told Paige. "He's a far better cook than Kellan. No offense."

"None taken." If Kellan had remembered the potluck was today, he'd have brought chicken tenders from the deli. Or maybe a salad. Nothing that required a recipe.

Paige didn't smile at the exchange, though,

and she stuck close to Trudie in the fellowship hall while they mingled with other parishioners. Once Benton arrived and said grace, she sat on the far side of her aunt during lunch, apparently still determined to keep a distance between herself and Kellan. When Kellan rose to grab another helping of food, Gran followed after him, unable to hide the disturbed set of her jaw.

"What is going on with you and Paige?"

"Nothing, Gran."

"Posh. You're in the middle of a lover's quarrel."

"Quarrel maybe, but there is nothing romantic going on between me and Paige."

"Don't fib, now. You two were holding hands in your office the other day. In a romantic and cozy pose."

What? He and Paige had never held hands—

Wait. She said it was the other day? In his office?

He rubbed his forehead. Gran was referring to the lip gloss incident.

"This story came from Jane? It couldn't have been anyone else."

Gran's cheeks pinked. "She didn't tell me, specifically."

Great. Small-town gossip at its finest. "Well, Jane misinterpreted what she saw. Paige smacked into me on accident and while our hands were technically touching at the moment Jane came into the office, there was no *holding* going on." He didn't dare mention the lip gloss on his shirt, or that would have been misinterpreted, too.

Gran's lower lip protruded. "Well, I am disappointed by this. We all will be."

How many times had he told her and his mom that he was not interested in dating? They never seemed to listen to him, and it rankled not to be taken seriously. "I know you mean well, but Paige and I are not involved, okay? And we're not going to be. I know you, Trudie and Marigold want to hear something different, but I can't help you there."

Her sniff conveyed her displeasure. "Well, you may not be interested in dating Paige, but it's time you made up from whatever argument you've had. Come to the cake table with me."

"Time to cut your cake?"

"Yes." But instead of picking up the knife, she waved her arm to get the attention of their table. "Paige? Paige, come here, please. My knee is giving me fits and I need to sit down. You and Kellan will cut the cake for me, won't you?"

Paige hopped right up, her brows knit in concern. "Of course, Eileen."

If Gran's knee was bothering her, she hadn't mentioned it. And she sure was smiling when she left them to the cake.

Paige picked up the cake knife. "Is this a case of the matchmakers striking again, just like with the bocce game?"

"Maybe not matchmaking, but they want us to make up. It's a ploy, for sure. Gran's not acting like she needs to sit down." On the contrary, Gran migrated to a cluster of standing women, linking arms with one and engaging in some spirited chatter.

"For what it's worth, Aunt Trudie was in the act of sending me here to help you with the cake when Eileen called me over." She sliced a perfectly square corner piece of chocolate cake, frosted with rich chocolate and scattered with walnuts, and set it on a paper plate.

Kellan placed a plastic fork on it and set it to the side. "The truth is, I'm glad they meddled this time and threw us together so I can say I'm sorry. I don't want to fight with you, Paige."

"We weren't fighting."

It sure seemed like it. She wanted him to confide in her, and he wouldn't. Couldn't. So she'd built a wall between them so high and wide, he didn't know how to get around it.

Or even if he should try. Maybe it would be better to leave the wall alone and not try to continue this conversation when there were fewer people around. If this disagreement or whatever it was ended their friendship, maybe it wouldn't hurt as much when she left town.

Adults and kids alike approached the cake table, so he couldn't respond to Paige, even if he knew what to say. He plated the squares Paige sliced, their movements rushed to keep up with the demand.

As things started to slow down, a small child with dark, curly hair appeared at Paige's side. Paige lowered her knife. "What's this? Do you have a book there?"

Sure enough, the girl held out a floppy white paperback. "Weed it," she insisted.

Oh, *read* it.

As Paige took the book, a woman about his age hurried to the table, hands going to the child's shoulders. "Sorry to bother you two. Mira said she knows you from her summer program, but I know that can't be right. I don't recognize you from Little Lambs."

"I don't teach there, no, but I did read to the three-year-olds during literacy week." Paige smiled at the mom before turning an even bigger smile on the little girl. "I remember you, too, Mira, and I'd be happy to read to you, if Mr. Lambert here doesn't mind handling the cake."

"What cake?" Hardly an eighth of it remained. "No problem."

"You have to sit on a chair." The little girl pointed to a vacant metal folding chair against the wall close to the cake table. "And I sit here." She dropped cross-legged to the speckled cream linoleum underfoot.

As Paige took her seat and glanced at the book, a few other children eyed her and Mira with unabashed curiosity. "Come and sit for a story," she invited.

They did, except for one boy who held a clear plastic cup of lemonade. He stood at Paige's side. "Let me see."

"I'll show the pictures to everyone, don't worry," Paige said with a firm sweetness that reminded Kellan once again how well-suited she was to teaching young ones. "Sit back down and I'll—"

The boy stumbled against her. Lemonade saturated her midsection and the plastic cup clattered to the floor. At once the boy burst into a wail loud and piercing as a police siren. Paige reached for him even as liquid dripped from her hem. Kellan grabbed the stack of thin napkins from the table and hurried over, but Trudie was faster.

Paige's great-aunt had the crying boy and the paperback in her hands before Kellan could offer the napkins to Paige. Her grateful glance told him she appreciated his help, but her words were soft and gentle for the boy. "Accidents happen. We can get you more lemonade."

Kellan's napkins were no match for the mess on the floor, and when he looked up, Trudie was shooing Paige from the chair. "I haven't read a book to little ones since you were this size. Go get cleaned up."

"Are you sure?"

"Paige." Trudie leveled her with a look. "I am perfectly capable of reading aloud to children."

Kellan offered Paige his hand and assisted her from the folding chair. "The restrooms are over there, if you want to get a damp paper towel. Or twelve."

She laughed, as he'd hoped. While Trudie started reading the story about a truck, he left the cake table—folks could cut their own squares if they wanted more—and found rags in the supply closet. He crouched behind Trudie to wipe up the sticky mess. They'd need a wet mop later, but this should work for now so no one would slip on the slick floor.

Paige exited the restroom, her yellow-and-white dress blotched and damp. He brought her a clean rag. "Less sticky now?"

"Some, thanks." She took the rag and blotted. "What's going on?"

"What do you mean?" He followed her gaze. Trudie had finished the book about the truck, and now stood with the once-crying boy in her arms, just behind the circle of children. Every little pair of eyes focused on Gran, who sat in the chair reading a story from a thick-paged children's Bible.

It wasn't just children who were enraptured, either. Several of Gran's friends, all senior citizens, approached as if they wanted to listen to the story.

Others stayed back and watched. "Aren't they sweet?" one older woman said.

"It's been so long since I've had a little one on my lap to read a story," her friend responded. "Eileen?" she called. "I'll take a turn when you're done."

"Would you look at that?" Paige gazed up at him, eyes sparkling with excitement and something else. Something like camaraderie, and it only intensified when she laid her fingertips on his arm. It was like they hadn't disagreed this morning. Like the boundary between them had fallen to rubble at their feet. "I've got an idea."

"Oh, yeah?" Friend or not, she was adorable when she was this excited.

And he had to admit being around her made him feel brighter, too.

"But before I go into all of that, I'm sorry for earlier. You apologized, and I didn't offer much of a response."

"Well, things did get busy at the cake table. We couldn't really talk."

"I should've acknowledged your apology and offered my own, though. I was still so consumed with frustration over my situation. Peanut seeming to get bigger overnight and 'hello, world, I'm having a baby' shouldn't have upset me as much as it did, but I know it's part of a larger picture. Everything has been somewhat overwhelming."

"I can only imagine."

She faced him squarely. "But you've been nothing but kind to me. I shouldn't have pushed you to talk to me about whatever it is that's bugging you, especially if you're not ready. I just want to help you like you've helped me. I'm sorry. Are we okay?"

"Of course we are, as long as you're okay. And I'm sorry I hurt you. That is truly the one thing I never want to do, Paige." He stared into her soulful eyes. "As far as helping goes, though, I hope you know you do help me. A lot."

"Not just at the store." She shook her head. "As a friend."

"You do that, too."

"Really?"

"Really. You make me laugh and lighten me up. You're fun to be around." He offered her the last piece of cake. "I wouldn't want to be set up by nosy matchmaking relatives with anyone else but you."

She laughed, but Kellan recognized more than a grain of truth in what he said. She was the only woman whom he truly wanted to spend time with. But he wasn't going to go down that road any further. "I want you to be happy and use your gifts, Paige. To grow into what God made you to do and be."

"Me, too." Her smile broadened. "Which brings me to a new idea." She gestured at the seniors and preschoolers in the corner, her eyes remarkable as they flashed in her excitement. "Here's what I'm thinking."

Whatever it was, it was bound to be amazing, and Kellan couldn't take his eyes off her.

Later that evening Paige relaxed in one of the blue padded chairs on Kellan's backyard patio, polishing off her second piece of pepperoni pizza. It was so relaxing, dining al fresco like this. Birdsong filled the warm, early-evening air, and a gentle breeze rocked the hanging porch swing. Water bubbled in the small fountain beside a chaise, where Frank perched, licking his front paws. Gladys patrolled around the bushes, trailed by little Sydney. Jet, however, lay at Paige's feet, his dark eyes wide and begging as if he hoped she'd let some pepperoni spill off her plate for him.

Paige sighed in contentment. "I'm glad you suggested dinner."

Kellan helped himself to a second round of the green salad she'd brought over. "Well, we both had to eat, didn't we? Why not share dinner while we worked out a proposal for your excellent idea?"

Paige's plan, inspired by the older folks reading to kids in the parish hall today, was to arrange for a reading buddy program between Little Lambs and Creekside Retirement Village. "I don't want to get my hopes up. They might not go for it."

"I don't know why not. A buddy program will be of social benefit to both groups, seniors and preschoolers. It promotes literacy. And it costs nothing. Open Book is happy to donate the reading materials. Trust me, Jane and Tanya will love it."

Tanya, she'd found out, was the name of the social director at Creekside. "I hope so, but they might not have room in their schedules."

"If it doesn't work for the summer program,

maybe Jane can do it in the autumn. I think it's great, Paige. Honest."

The crinkled set of his eyes told her he meant it. "Thanks, Kellan. So what do you think I should—oh, hello." Little Sydney bit into Paige's loose flip-flop, gnawing at the soft, rubbery sole.

"Don't do that, Sydney." Kellan urged her away.

"That must feel good to a teething puppy."

"She's chewed pretty much everything she's encountered since I brought her home." Kellan offered Sydney a bedraggled-looking rope toy. "I've never had a puppy before."

"No? Not these guys?" She reached to pat Jet's head.

"Fully grown when I got them." Kellan swallowed the last of his iced tea. "Gladys belonged to an elderly neighbor who passed away. The family suffers bad allergies, so I took her in. She's a senior dog, and I worried she wouldn't be happy with the transition."

"She looks pretty happy to me." Gladys lay on the grass near Frank, mouth open so it almost looked like she smiled. "And Jet?"

The dog lifted his head at the mention of his name, so Paige rubbed his brow again.

"He was hit by a car about two years ago and lost his leg. No one claimed him, and rather than send him to the shelter, the vet called me to see if I knew of anyone who might want him. But one look at him, and I was sold. Named him Jet because despite only having three legs, he's still pretty fast when there's food involved. No idea how old he is, five or six? But Frank is four. One of Marigold's friends found his mama and litter in her garden shed. I helped find homes for all of them, but I kept Frank, obviously."

"So you didn't go looking for any of these guys, did you?" As if his hiring her and granting her shelter wasn't enough, now she knew Kellan's heart was pure gold.

"You know that saying, they rescued me more than the other way around? It's true. They've been good for me."

"I haven't had a pet in a long time." Not since Muffin, a Yorkie, passed away when she was in high school.

"Well, these guys are certainly happy to stand in as substitutes."

"I like that idea." Sydney sniffed around her flip-flop again, but Paige didn't mind. She was such a cute puppy, it was hard to mind anything she did.

And Paige didn't feel much like moving, not on such a beautiful evening. She didn't even want to get up and clear away the pizza box and dishes, because she might never get back this same sense of relaxation and peace. So she ignored the mess on the table and discussed her idea for the buddy program with Kellan, answering his questions, asking a few of her own, taking notes in the small spiral-bound notebook she'd brought over.

Talk flowed to the bookstore, how sales of local books and viewings of the anvil in the museum case had increased since he moved the bookshelf and opened the space. Paige's thoughts gravitated to the people she encountered in the store.

"I was hoping to see Mickey or Herb at church. Or some other people I've met."

"Mickey attends the church south of the creek, same as Faith and Tom. I don't think Herb goes anywhere. I've invited him to come with me, but he never does. I wish he would, for a lot of reasons, but one of them would be to meet people. He's lonely."

"He mentioned he was stationed in Germany in the army. I wonder if he'd benefit from something like that veterans' group in Pinehurst."

"He might. Maybe we can bring it up with him tomorrow." He tapped the table with his forefinger. "And let's order that rug for Toddler

Story Time. It won't be here by our next meeting Wednesday, but maybe by the next week."

She clapped. "The kids will love it."

"Which reminds me, Mickey's got an appointment Wednesday. Would you mind taking on Toddler Story Time?"

"You don't have to ask me twice." At once she thought of the books she'd read, one of which described a dance she and the kids could do.

"You're perfect for it, Paige. Thanks."

"I'm the one who should be thanking you." She sighed. "We're always thanking each other."

"Maybe we're grateful."

Yes, but there was more to it, on her side, anyway. He supported her, encouraged her, for who she was, not who someone else thought she should be.

Being seen for who she was? What a rare thing, indeed.

Watching him scoop Sydney from the patio and place her on his lap, she liked to think she saw him for who he was, too.

A beautiful, kind heart.

Chapter Twelve

The following week and a half passed in a busy hum of activity for Paige. She and Kellan visited Faith's antiques store and chose a distressed red armoire from which to display the educational toys that Kellan had ordered. They set up the sales display on the second floor, along with the new rug she'd chosen, nonskid and kid friendly. She might have been biased, but both the rug and the toys seemed to be big hits.

Paige also pitched her idea for the reading buddy program, fully expecting Jane at Little Lambs to say *no*, or *not now*. Summer program schedules were usually booked up far in advance, but she hoped maybe Jane would like the idea for a future time, at least.

It turned out Jane's programming had fallen through for the next week, when a dentist who'd been on the books to give a presentation about brushing habits had to cancel. "An outing to Creekside would be wonderful," Jane said. "I love the idea of a reading buddy program. As long as it works for Creekside, it works for us."

Tanya, the tiny, sable-haired social director at Creekside, agreed before Paige could even complete her pitch. "We're in."

Just like he'd promised, Kellan provided the books. "Anything you want." He'd gestured to the second floor of the store.

And now, here she was, ten days after discussing her idea with Kellan on his back patio, standing in the Creekside lobby, praying under her breath as the preschoolers, teachers and parent volunteers arrived from their walk from Little Lambs. The senior residents who'd volunteered to pair up with a three-or four-year-old waited in the lounge, eager to read stories and then enjoy a light snack and make a simple craft together.

This could either flop or be wonderful. *Please, Lord, let it be wonderful.*

The children filed past, wearing name tags that dangled from brightly hued lanyards about their little necks. A few of the kids, including Mira from church, saw her and waved. She waved back.

Too bad Kellan couldn't have come with her today, but he'd had to stay at Open Book for a prescheduled meeting with his stepdad, Don. She snapped a few photos on her phone to share with him when she returned to work. Several of Eileen with her little buddy, a boy wearing a fringed, Western-style vest, and some of Trudie, too, paired with a redheaded girl with bright freckles. Both ladies looked incandescently taken with their buddies.

Once the story time got going, Jane moseyed over to Paige. "They all look so happy."

"They do, don't they?" Some of the little ones even snuggled into the older folks' sides, a lovely sight, but one that reminded Paige that soon, she'd have a little one of her own snuggling against her.

"Tanya and I hope to repeat this event, maybe even make it a regular program. She said the residents were clamoring to sign up and spend time with the kids. Some of them don't get many visits from their own loved ones, much less news or phone calls. They miss being part of their families' lives. So sad, isn't it?"

Families missing out on news…news like a new baby? A lump filled Paige's throat. How could she not think of her decision not to tell her own mother about Peanut?

Paige's hand went to her stomach.

She'd thought she was doing the right thing, waiting to tell Mom about Peanut until she had a solid plan. That way, Mom wouldn't be able to chide her for a lack of self-sufficiency. To protect herself from that uncomfortable discussion, though, Paige had denied her mother all the little joys that came along with her pregnancy. The kicks, the growth and even a copy of the ultrasound picture she'd framed and propped on the table in the tiny house.

Would Mom feel like she'd been prevented from being part of the baby's life? If the tables were turned, Paige would be hurt. Achingly so.

Should she tell Mom? Right now?

She could practically hear Kellan telling her, *It's your decision. I'll support you whatever you do.*

But she couldn't help wonder what God thought of her decision to wait.

Lord, I want to be a good daughter. That's why I'm waiting to share the news, so Mom won't be so disappointed in me. But what would please You?

Jane took a half step closer, dragging Paige's attention to the present. "So how long have you and Kellan been seeing each other?"

A weird noise escaped Paige's throat. "We're not—we aren't dating."

"Oops. I was mistaken." Jane's red eyebrows rose. "You guys looked chummy, with the hand-holding, that's all."

Hand-holding? When had they ever held hands? They'd hugged that one time in the alley, but no one saw them, did they? When had Jane been around? Oh, yeah—when she'd blotted the lip gloss off his shirt.

"We're, um, chums." Couldn't she think of anything better to say? "He knew my brother in the army."

"Maybe that explains your camaraderie. You've known him a long time."

Four years of acquaintance, really, but she didn't feel like explaining to Jane. Especially about Drew.

"It's kind of cute, how excited he is for you taking online classes. Last night he said you'd started yesterday?"

She had, after work, watching a lecture on her computer. But right now her brain fixed on Jane having seen Kellan last night. Paige shouldn't care a spoonful of beans if Kellan was rethinking his "staying single" thing, with Jane or anyone else, but she did. "He told you about my classes?"

"Last night at a cycling club meeting. He also told me he got a new puppy. Have you seen it?"

Oh, yes, cycling club. And hadn't Kellan told her he wasn't interested in Jane? None of her business, but those two facts made Paige's shoulders relax. "Sydney, yes. She's adorable."

"A mutt?"

"Part Australian shepherd, we think, and part corgi. Her legs are so short, but she runs to keep up with the big dogs. It's cute."

"What number of rescue animal is this for him? He can't say no to a stray, can he?" Jane laughed. "It's like he's addicted to rescue projects. Something needs help, and he steps right in."

Paige's laugh sounded strangled to her ears. Was that what she was to Kellan? A rescue project?

Okay first, she wasn't a dog or a cat. She was the sister of one of his friends who'd been lost in Afghanistan.

And second, what did it matter if Kellan viewed her like a stray animal needing a home? Sure, he'd said they were friends, but friendship meant different things to different people. And of course, there were different types of friendships. Lifelong friends were rare, and something Paige had never experienced herself. Her longest-lasting relationships shifted in their degrees of closeness over time. Other friendships she'd had were temporary, fulfilling a purpose for a finite period of time.

This was probably like that for him. She might have sensed that they liked each other, but they'd both been clear that they had no interest in being in relationships. She'd made the choice to stay single and raise Peanut herself, right? So why, at the thought of being a project to Kellan, did her rib cage ache with something resembling regret?

As much fun as this was, coming up with an event for the preschool, it was a distraction from her plan. She needed to buckle down and spend some serious time in prayer tonight. Widow's Peak Creek was not her home. She needed to figure things out so she could tell her mother about Peanut and get her life back on track.

As Kellan pored over financials with Don at the office conference table, he couldn't help but watch the clock. Paige should be back soon. How did the reading buddy program go? She was so good at this thing. She'd be an incredible preschool teacher.

Don's tapping pencil demanded Kellan's attention. "So you can see if we have two more good months, there'll be plenty of cushion in the budget to look at properties for the second store in Pinehurst."

Kellan rubbed his forehead. "You know I'm not on the same page as when it comes to opening a second store, Don."

Don blinked, his eyes small behind his thick glasses. "Your reticence doesn't make a lick of sense, Kellan. Business sense or common sense. Pinehurst is similar in population and demographic to Widow's Peak Creek, with a long history. It's close enough to the highway that tourists stop in. Most important, though, Pinehurst doesn't have a bookstore. Those folks have to order books online or drive to a big-box store in Sacramento. They'd be delighted to support an independent bookstore that employs their people. It's a win-win."

"I don't dispute the benefits of Pinehurst having its own bookstore, Don. I'm just not sure it needs to be us running that store. I never set out to grow into a franchise. You know that. I'd rather reinvest the profits in local programs."

"Pinehurst has local programs that could use investing in, too. Your mother was telling me the veterans' group there has a bookroom that's practically empty. She said there were a few books on veterans' issues, but the people who hang out there want some fiction, too. You could help with that."

"I'm happy to donate books, and I don't need a store in Pinehurst to do it. But I'm guessing Mom wasn't inside the veterans' hall because she wanted to do an inventory of their library." He rubbed his aching forehead. "Obviously, she's checking out groups for me."

He was grateful for her love but annoyed at the same time.

"She's just trying to help." Don shrugged, clearly not too worried about the situation. He was obviously more interested in opening a second store, because he shoved a spreadsheet over to Kellan's side of the table. "Here, this will cheer you up. My projections show we could make a mint. And that's why you connected with me in the first place, because of my money sense."

"I wanted to survive our first year and I knew you'd know how to navigate the pitfalls small businesses face. I was right. But as you recall, I also told you on day one that I wanted to be a resource to the community. To give back."

"Then give back to Pinehurst as well as Widow's Peak Creek. As for me, I'll use my first paycheck to take your mother on an Alaskan cruise. She's worked hard all her life, and deserves to be pampered, don't you think?"

"Of course she does." Kellan didn't begrudge her that.

Don opened a manila file. "Now, let's talk about sales. Looking good, with an uptick in interest in books on local history and kids' books. And what's this with orders?"

"Paige read a book to the kids during story time last week that proved to be popular. Several of the parents wanted to purchase copies, and we ran out."

"We'll have to plan for that in the future, have multiple copies of the books that get read."

"It hasn't happened before, but Paige is good with the kids. She picked a book with some sort of dance described in it and got everyone moving."

Don had lost interest, drawing Kellan's attention to payroll.

Twenty minutes later they'd finished, but Kellan felt as drained as if he'd cycled twenty miles. It was like he and Don spoke two different languages these days, and he was frustrated when he made his way to the kitchenette to refill his water bottle. Paige, wearing a loose dress in a peach hue that complemented her hair and rosy cheeks, stood at the sink, rinsing a plump yellow apple.

At once, his spirits brightened. "Hey. I didn't know you'd come back from Creekside. How'd it go?"

"Really well, from my view. I think they'll continue the program." She shook water from the apple. "Your grandma looked like she was having a nice time with her little buddy. I took pictures."

"I'm eager to see them."

"What's that?" Her gaze was on his hand as she bit into her apple.

Ugh, he still held the spreadsheet Don made up projecting profits if they opened a second store. He folded it in quarters and shoved it into his pants pocket. "Don's push to expand Open Book to Pinehurst. He's not giving up."

She swallowed her bite of apple. "It sounds like he's had that as his agenda for a while, though, hasn't he?"

"He sees it as a ticket to profit, yeah. There's nothing wrong with wealth, of course. It's how we relate to it, what we do with it, that complicates things." He refilled his water bottle as he spoke. "But neither Don nor Mom are believers, so we view money differently. That and pretty much everything else. So Don doesn't understand that I'm not interested in expanding my book empire," he joked.

She stared at her apple. "Peanut's dad was—is—kind of like that. Like Don. Interested in accumulating wealth."

She hadn't talked about the baby's father in a while. Maybe she needed to. "Yeah? How so?"

"Aidan is obsessed with his stock portfolio. It didn't start out that way. He's a computer coder and when I met him, he loved what he did. It was like a kid at play for him. But toward the end of our relationship, he started talking about driving the 'right' kind of car and having the latest tech. Nothing about whether or not he was happy with the work. Don't get me wrong, we've all got to make a living, right? But I don't need stuff like that to make me happy."

Her smile didn't reach her eyes. Did she miss Peanut's dad? It was none of his business, but he had to know.

"Do you still love him? Aidan?"

Her gaze fixed on the floor. "When he sent me those papers signing away parental rights? That right there killed any tenderness between us. I thought it was love, but the pain I felt after he left was betrayal. Not the ache of lost love." She lifted her eyes then. "Strange as it might sound, I'm grateful that he backed out of our lives. I don't want Peanut to ever feel unwanted or lied to."

Kellan's stomach tightened. *Lied to.* The words echoed through his core.

He was lying to Paige. Every minute of every day, he was withholding the truth about Drew's death from her, lying by omission. He kept quiet to protect her, although right now it felt like he was lying to protect himself.

That's not true. I was instructed to let sleeping dogs lie.

He set down his water bottle, arguing with himself. *Instructed, not ordered. I wouldn't be breaking any rules telling Paige and her mom our squad ended up on that road because of me.*

Kellan scrubbed his forehead with his hand, as if he could banish the memory from his brain of that awful day when Drew died.

"What's wrong?" Paige's voice sounded far away.

He shook off his fog of memories. "Sorry. I was listening. I'm glad you're not grieving the loss of your relationship with Aidan."

"Are you sure you're okay?" Her tone was less suspicious than it was concerned. "You're pale and your hand is shaking."

Was it? He shoved it in his pocket.

"Something's bothering you."

"I'm bothered that Peanut's dad left you both like he did."

Her level gaze told him she didn't believe him. "I can tell something's off, Kellan, and it's not just that. You've done this before with me, like I say something that upsets you and you aren't telling me. Please let me make it right. Let me help you."

She couldn't. No one could. God's word said to bear one another's burdens, but this particular load?

He'd hurt her if he shared it.

Unless—unless he was hurting her more by not telling her the truth. She and her mom deserved to know how Drew died, didn't they?

He was tempted to tell her. Tempted by the relief that honesty always brought, even when the truth stung. And oh, how this truth would inflict damage with its barbs. And she would hate him. He'd lose her from his life forever. He rubbed his aching forehead, praying for wisdom. Fast.

A thump hit the floor, like a tennis ball smacking the hardwood. Paige's half-eaten apple wobbled past his foot. His head snapped up. She bent forward, face down, hands at her stomach.

"Paige?" He took gentle hold of her upper arms in case her legs went out from under her.

"It's okay. Just—hurts."

"Sit down." He guided her to the small table where the employees sat for breaks.

"I'm fine." She didn't look it as she settled into one of the folding chairs. "It's just like last time I had a pain, remember? This is nothing but ligaments."

Relief flooded his veins, chasing the adrenaline that had started pumping double time. "It's the same type of pain?"

"Kind of."

That wasn't the answer he'd hoped for. He still crouched before her chair, staring at her face, gauging for signs of pain or distress. "You had both hands on your stomach. Last time it was one side that hurt. Do you want to call the doctor? Are you still seeing the same one?"

"Yes, but no need to call. It's better now."

What if he'd caused this by upsetting her? "Did I stress you out?"

"Don't be ridiculous." Her lips crooked up in a half smile. "In fact, I'm ready to get back to work."

If she said so. At times like this his roles as boss and friend blurred, but the most important thing in either aspect of their relationship was her well-being. He stood so she could rise. "If something changes, though, just say the word."

"I will, but I'm fine. The worst part is I dropped my apple. It was a good one, too." She bent to scoop it off the ground as if demonstrating how fabulous she felt. "I meant what I said, Kellan. I want to help you."

"Thanks, Paige. I'm just not ready. Is that okay?"

"It is. Everything's A-okay." She seemed relieved that at least he'd admitted something was bothering him.

Half an hour later, though, she didn't look at all relieved or okay when Kellan passed by the history section. She curved into one of the shelves, her head down, her grip white-knuckled on the top shelf.

"Paige?"

Her eyes were red when she met his gaze. "The pain. It's coming every five minutes."

Every five minutes. For half an hour. And she wasn't due to deliver for months.

Kellan didn't know much about babies, but he knew this wasn't good.

"I'll grab my keys."

Chapter Thirteen

The sharp odor of industrial disinfectant filled the ER waiting room, so strong that Kellan could see the Bagram hospital where he was treated for his gunshot wound, even with his eyes wide open. He breathed through his mouth. In, out. *Focus on something specific. The hum of the fluorescent lights overhead. The orange splotch on the tile.*

Better yet, pray for Paige.

Every prayer he'd started since bringing her to the WPC Community Hospital, though, had ended with a silent cry of helplessness, a plea for Paige and her baby. Would his unspoken, wordless cries of the heart be heard by God?

Of course they would. He knew that. There was that verse in Romans about the Spirit helping us in our weakness and interceding for us. Kellan clung to it now. It was almost impossible to articulate a prayer, worried as he was about Paige and the baby, all while triggered by disinfectant and shoving down memories of Drew's death and its aftermath.

Maybe he should wait outside and get away from the smells, along with the press of people crowding into the waiting room. He didn't want to go too far, though, in case Paige returned or, more likely, a nurse came to give him an update. Paige said she'd text when she knew something, but just in case she couldn't get to her phone, he didn't want to be out of sight.

He checked his phone again. Nothing. The only text he'd received in the forty-five minutes since she'd been taken back to an examination room was a check-in from Marigold. He'd informed her that Paige was experiencing what they thought could be labor and her doctor had sent her straight to the emergency room. He'd asked her to please tell Gran, who didn't have a cell phone, and Trudie. He didn't have her number, and he wasn't sure Paige was in any condition to text her great-aunt.

They were all praying for Paige, he was sure of it. Mickey was, too, and even Herb said he'd pray. In a rush of blessing, Kellan gave thanks for everyone who had come alongside Paige and even now lifted her and Peanut to the Lord.

*Thank You for giving us one another, Lord.
Thank you for that fellowship.*

Well, look at that. He'd finished a prayer and
avoided thinking of Afghanistan for the past
two minutes. That was a victory right there.

His phone buzzed again. His pulse hitched,
but it was Marigold again, not Paige.

Where are you?

What did she mean by that? He'd told her
he was at the ER. He started to type out a response when something made him look up.
Three older women paused inside the auto-
matic doors, scanning the crowd filling the
waiting room.

He hopped to his feet. At seeing him, Trudie
shut her eyes in relief, Marigold clapped her
hands to her chest and Gran bustled toward
him with her usual brisk efficiency. As she
hugged him, she tutted. "It's packed in here."

"Typical emergency room," Trudie said,
shaking her head.

Kellan offered the ladies his seat. There
weren't any others free in here. They argued
politely before Gran sat down, purse in her lap.

"No news yet," he said.

Trudie laced her arm through his. "We came

to keep you company until we can all be with Paige."

"And pray," Marigold added.

He hugged Trudie, then Marigold, before reaching to squeeze Gran's hand. "Thank you for coming."

"Kellan Lambert?" a female voice called from behind him. He swiveled to face a woman in maroon scrubs in the threshold to the triage area.

"Yes." He raised his hand so she'd know he was coming, but he beckoned Trudie to come with him. "I'll see if you can go in, instead."

But when he asked, the woman shook her head. "I was given your name, sir. No one else is invited back unless the patient authorizes you two to switch out."

He glanced at Trudie. "It's because she doesn't know you're here. I'll let her know so you and I can switch."

"Just go, Kellan." Trudie waved him away. "Take care of our Paigey."

Our Paigey. That was what she was, wasn't she? She was loved by all of them. She was a part of them.

A part of my life and my heart.

The thought dissipated under the strong fumes of disinfectant as he followed the nurse down the hall, past a staff member tending the linoleum floor with a mop and bucket. *That right there. That's the smell from the hospital after Drew died—*

Not now. *Focus on Paige.*

The nurse pushed back a pale green curtain to allow him into a cubicle. Paige propped on a narrow bed, her eyes rimmed red, but she had a small smile for him. "It's okay now. It's over and Peanut and I are both fine."

He dropped into the chair beside the bed and took her hand in both of his, carefully avoiding the IV needle stuck in the back of her hand. "Are you sure?"

"Yes and no. I mean, Dr. Graves was able to stop the labor—"

"So it actually was labor. Not ligaments again." Kellan's stomach turned inside out.

"No, it was the real deal. Way too early." Paige's free hand caressed her tummy. "I'm only six months along."

"Thank God they could stop it." He pressed a kiss onto her knuckles.

A petite, black-haired woman around forty entered the cubicle, introducing herself as Dr. Graves.

"Mickey's cousin." Kellan shook her hand but immediately returned his hold on Paige's fingers.

"Yes, she's my baby cousin. And speaking

of babies, yours is doing well, Paige. Excellent heart rate, no signs of distress whatsoever. In fact, this little one has been rather active since the contractions ended." She tucked a strand of her bobbed hair behind her ear. "I'm glad I was in the hospital and could tend to you personally. Although the other doctors here are excellent, of course."

Now that they were talking about sensitive things like contractions, maybe Kellan should go. "Trudie's here. Do you want her in here instead of me?"

Paige shook her head. "You can stay. If you don't mind, of course."

"I don't." He grazed his lips against her knuckles again to prove it.

Dr. Graves scanned the chart. "Then let's talk about what to expect when you go home. Bedrest is no longer unilaterally prescribed after experiencing preterm labor, and I don't see the need for you to be confined to bed, so you may resume many of your regular activities. Try to vary your position between standing and sitting. Low-impact exercise is fine. And avoid all stress."

Kellan's heart dropped to his gut. "Did stress cause this?"

"Many times, we don't know what causes preterm labor. We want to play it safe, though."

She ran down a list of things she wanted Paige to do, including receiving adequate rest, eating well and so forth.

Kellan squeezed Paige's fingers. *Thank You, God. For stopping labor and protecting the baby. For stopping me from telling Paige the truth about Drew, since it could have made this situation so much worse.* He'd been so tempted to when she questioned him in the kitchenette. But this was his burden to bear. He would not do anything to jeopardize Paige or Peanut's health again.

Which is why he traded off with Trudie while Paige got ready to come home, taking the opportunity to shoot a text to Benton, his pastor. His friend.

Free to meet tomorrow?

Benton's reply was swift.

Sure. Good coffee at Angel Food Bakery or my bad coffee at the church office?

This was definitely a matter for the church office.

Then he texted Mickey and filled her in on Paige's situation, asking if she could close the store for him tonight. Once he received her thumbs-up emoji, he used the hospital Wi-Fi to get on his preferred source to order books. By the time Paige was ready to go home, he'd ordered a dozen books on pregnancy—not for the bookstore, but for him.

He had to know all he could to better help Paige.

"No more bocce for you." Aunt Trudie opened every cupboard but one in the kitchen of Paige's tiny house once they returned from the hospital. "Where are your drinking glasses?"

"The one cupboard that's still closed," Paige teased as she set down her purse. "Here, I'll—"

"Sit down, missy." Aunt Trudie pointed at the recliner. "You promised Kellan you'd put your feet up when you got home, and you don't want me to get in trouble when he gets here." He, Eileen and Marigold were coming for a light dinner of Aunt Trudie's famous tuna sandwiches.

"I don't like sitting like a bump on a log while you're working, though." But she sat. "You know, Dr. Graves said I still need exercise."

"Humor us, dear." Aunt Trudie poured orange juice into the glass and carried it to her. "We just want you and the baby to be all right."

She thanked Aunt Trudie for the juice and took a small sip. "Trust me, I'll do whatever I have to do to keep Peanut healthy."

As she finished her juice, the odor of tuna fish filled her small living area. Aunt Trudie's tuna salad recipe was famous in their family, dappled with dill weed and crunchy with celery. "Thanks for dinner, Aunt Trudie."

"Oh, this is fun. Even though I have a kitchenette in my condo, I don't cook much anymore. It's more fun to eat with everyone else in the dining room. Eileen feels the same way. She and I chose to move to Creekside for the social stuff." She sighed. "As my darling Chuck used to say, life throws curveballs but we still have to stay in the game until all the innings are up."

"He sure loved baseball." And baseball metaphors. Uncle Chuck had been gone ten years now, but he had been just as kind as Aunt Trudie.

Of course, Paige had her own motto. *There's a blue sky behind those dark clouds.* Although she hadn't been thinking about it much lately, and right now, looking at her life, the clouds seemed pretty thick and impenetrable.

Since Dr. Graves didn't want her on her feet all day, Paige probably couldn't keep her job at Open Book. She had enough money set aside to live on, if she was frugal, but the extra income she received from working at the store was a blessing right now.

She had to put Peanut's health first, though.

Perhaps it was wrong to feel anything other than gratitude that she and the baby were safe, but disappointment shrouded her like a blanket. Disappointment in her circumstances, and in herself. How could her body betray her like this? Why did she go into labor three months early? Had she done something wrong, or was there something wrong with her?

Well, the answers to those last questions were obvious. Of course. She was single, pregnant and relying on the kindness of others.

Her mom would deem her a failure. A failure without a plan.

Paige plucked at a piece of lint on her dress. "I was thinking maybe I've been wrong not to tell Mom about Peanut. She'll be hurt to have been left out of the loop."

"You had your reasons, though. And I know Joyce. I understand why you'd want some distance."

A lot of distance, actually. Paige still preferred to have a plan before she talked to her mother. Frantically, her brain scrambled as if she could formulate one right now. Her online courses only lasted a month. That left her another two months before Peanut's official due date. She couldn't apply for preschool jobs until she'd finished her classes, gone through the security protocols and all of that, but where would she go? Back to Sacramento?

It no longer felt like home. That was one reason she'd come to Widow's Peak Creek in the first place.

I'm trying, God. I want to be a good mother and a woman who follows You, but right now I don't know what that even means. Where do I go from here?

"Knock knock." Marigold's voice preceded her into the little house. She was followed by Eileen, carrying a caddy of cleaning supplies, and Kellan, his arms laden with grocery bags. Paige stood to help, but Aunt Trudie pointed at the recliner like Paige was a dog learning the command to sit. "Let us do this, please."

"You don't need to, though." She was supposed to do everything by herself. And she was capable.

"But we *want* to." Eileen squinted at the furniture as if looking for dust. Paige kept the place tidy, but Eileen took a rag to the top of the television, anyway, before moving on to polish the banister of the spiral staircase.

Paige met Kellan's gaze, but couldn't decipher the silent message in his eyes before

Marigold moved in front of him. She held out a bouquet of Iceland poppies, salmon, peach and yellow in hue, arranged in an old-fashioned, clear glass milk bottle. "I brought your favorites, dear Paige."

"They're lovely." As Marigold set them down on the small dining table, the poppy heads bobbed on their thin, hairy stems as if they were waving hello. The sight always cheered her.

Thank You for every blessing, Lord. Small as well as large.

Marigold sighed as she adjusted the flowers. "These are the last of them for the season, I'm afraid. It's too hot for them to last."

"They're so pretty." Aunt Trudie added a squeeze of fresh lemon juice to the tuna salad. "I never knew they were your favorites, Paigey. I've always admired poppies. They're a flower with gumption."

"Gumption?" Kellan unpacked a grocery bag—oh, he'd picked up her favorite flavors of yogurt, the *right* brand of pickles and some deli salads.

Paige grinned at him but her words were for her aunt. "Yeah, explain the gumption to us."

"Have you ever noticed golden poppies grow alongside the road, as well as more picturesque spots? I like that our official state flower is not only pretty, but also hearty, thriving in some of the most hardscrabble places." Aunt Trudie peered over Kellan's shoulder into the fridge. "Celery, please."

He handed her the stalks, bound together by a shiny blue twist tie. "You know, you're right. They add a bit of sunshine to every landscape they find themselves in, whether it's a lush mountainside or a rocky path."

Paige sipped her juice. Was she something like those poppies, surviving in whatever type of soil she found herself? She'd been in lonely, dry soil at times in her past. But right now she was planted in an unexpected place of warmth and nurturing.

Watching her four uninvited but most welcome houseguests bustle about, she felt at once unable to care for herself—unable to be self-sufficient—but at the same time, blessed. How could she deny God had brought her here to these loving, faithful people?

For a season, of course. While she figured things out. Was that season almost at its end? Her life would look different now that she'd experienced preterm labor—how, she wasn't yet sure. She wasn't sure about anything, though. God hadn't yet answered her plea for direction.

Her gaze fell on Kellan, busy chopping celery. He'd told her sometimes, trust was a moment-by-moment decision. This was another one of those moments for her.

When I chose to follow You, Lord, I didn't know where You'd lead me, but I said I'd do my best to trust You. Help me live out that decision.

God didn't answer her with a plan, but she looked at her four visitors and remembered her motto. There was indeed a blue sky beyond the dark clouds. Right here was part of it, in four people who cared about her.

Marigold disappeared into the bathroom with a warning look that said "don't fight me, I'm cleaning your bathroom." Eileen finished with the banister and moved upstairs. Aunt Trudie spooned mayonnaise into the bowl of tuna.

And Kellan smiled at her with that high-wattage, infectious smile that had the power to knock a woman off her feet. Good thing she was already sitting down.

He held up two loaves of bread. "White or wheat for your sandwich?"

She had to clear the pounding lump of her heart out of her throat before she could speak. "Wheat, please."

"It's ready, so come load up," Aunt Trudie announced. "Marigold? Where'd you go? Stop dusting, Eileen, and come down here."

"Almost done." Eileen's voice carried from the loft as Marigold reemerged from the bathroom, accompanied by the odor of glass cleaner. Once they'd all assembled, Aunt Trudie prayed over their makeshift meal.

"Here you go." Kellan brought Paige a plate heaped high with broccoli salad from the deli, potato chips, a dill pickle spear and a tuna sandwich cut on the diagonal. Oh, boy, was her stomach rumbling. She hadn't eaten since breakfast, and Peanut was suddenly nudging her as if telling her to hurry up and eat.

"Thanks so much." She glanced at Kellan as she dug in. Delicious. "Aunt Trudie, your tuna salad's the *best*."

Kellan plopped on the love seat adjacent to her as the other ladies gathered around the small kitchen table. "I've got to try for myself."

As he took a large bite of his sandwich, Paige crunched into her pickle. It might be cliché, but she didn't care. It tasted fantastic to this pregnant lady. "Thanks for replenishing my pickle stock."

"I can't have you dipping low." He took a sip of water. "So here's the thing."

"There's a *thing*?"

"Yeah. See, I'm not comfortable with you being on your feet all day in the bookstore. Dr. Graves said you should vary your position, and it gave me a thought. Don and I are behind on data entry for several reports. We'd talked about hiring someone short term to handle it for us. Would you pray about switching to that job? Same pay, hours, whatever you need, and you wouldn't be standing all day. But there's a drawback. It would be lonelier work, confined to the office. Not that you couldn't move around. In fact, I'd expect you to take frequent breaks, to obey doctor's orders."

"This sounds too good to be true, Kellan. You're not making this up?"

"Nope. It's all true, Paige. When you see the how much data entry there is, you'll know it's no lie."

Eileen lifted her hand. "That reminds me of something. When Kellan was in elementary school, he played George Washington in a school play. He chopped down a fake little cherry tree and said 'I cannot tell a lie.' I have a photo of him in his costume of knickers and a white wig."

"How cute," Marigold said.

"I wouldn't mind seeing that picture." Paige took another bite of sandwich.

"Never." Kellan picked out a potato chip from his plate. "So, anyway, the job is something to consider, if you want to switch. You'd be helping me out."

"Helping each other, by the sounds of it." Marigold scrunched her shoulders.

Earlier today Jane from the preschool had called the stray animals Kellan's rescue projects. Paige may be something of a rescue project herself, but as he teased his grandma about cutting the crusts off her sandwich, and Eileen teased him back about leaving his crusts uneaten as a kid, Paige couldn't help but think of all the ways Kellan was a wonderful person all around. A loving grandson and son, although his mom and stepdad pushed his buttons. He still loved them. He was a giving friend. As if to prove it, he leaned toward her. "Need seconds of anything?"

"The salad, if there's any left."

"Absolutely." He rose. "Did I tell you Sydney likes broccoli?"

"The puppy?" Eileen's brows rose. "I don't think you're supposed to feed broccoli to dogs."

"Well, I dropped a piece on accident, and she gobbled it up. It wasn't a whole spear or anything." Kellan continued the story and Paige's thoughts returned to the job he'd offered her. It would be perfect.

Too perfect, as she'd told him. Yet once again, Kellan was providing the right opportunity at the right time.

Why do you view gifts and blessings with suspicion?

Because she'd been hurt, that was why. Hurt and lied to, which was how she found herself in Widow's Peak Creek in the first place. Taking self-protective measures against future pain was a normal, rational response.

But Kellan didn't deserve her mistrust, did he? He had demonstrated his faithful friendship over and over again. His calm, quick action got her to the hospital today before things got worse, and his concern had been real. There'd been no faking the fear in his eyes, not just for her, but Peanut, too.

He'd even kissed her hand a few times, he was so alarmed over what was happening to her.

She would not read anything into those chaste, quick kisses, even though they'd moved her, comforted her. They made her feel like someone truly cared for her and Peanut.

Kellan brought back her plate with a mound of sweet broccoli salad on it. "Let me know about the job switch when you come back to work. I figure you should take tomorrow off."

"No, I don't need to. And I'll do it. It would be a real help to me, Kellan. Thanks."

"Thank you." He smiled. Really smiled, that

wide, beaming grin of his that gave her arrhythmia.

Her attraction to him frightened her. Not just because she didn't want to be in a relationship, but also because that pull she had for him could only lead to deeper feelings. Which required trust.

Trouble.

Kellan was a special man. The best man she'd ever had the privilege to meet. But she had larger goals in mind, a baby to protect and provide for. She mustn't let down her guard.

Maybe it would be better just to enjoy the moment and be glad she wouldn't stay in Widow's Peak Creek long enough to be further tempted to care for him. To trust him.

Trusting only led to pain.

Chapter Fourteen

The next morning Kellan poured himself a cup of fresh-brewed coffee from the pot in the church office lobby. "Thanks for meeting me so early, Benton."

"It's not *that* early. I was up for my morning run, anyway." Grabbing his own full mug emblazoned with the church's blue logo, Benton led Kellan down the hall to his office, flicking on light switches as they went. He glanced at the white paper bag in Kellan's hand. "What do you have there?"

"Bear claws." Kellan had picked up his friend's favorite pastries from Angel Food Bakery on the way in. Once they were in Benton's office, he handed over the bag.

Benton claimed a pastry with almond paste oozing out the sides. "These are the best. Have a seat."

Kellan dropped into one of two well-worn, salmon-colored upholstered chairs in Benton's office. This early in the day, the church office was otherwise empty, so quiet he could hear the hum of the fluorescent lights and the continued drip of the coffeepot out in the lobby. It felt strange to be here when it wasn't humming with activity, but at the same time, the quiet was comforting.

Like he was free to speak whatever was on his mind.

It helped that Benton was a friend, not just his pastor. He and Kellan cycled together on occasion, had hiked and fished and prayed for one another. And he was the only person in town who knew Kellan was responsible for a squad member's death in Afghanistan. Paige's brother.

Benton placed his bear claw on a brown paper napkin. "So your text said Paige's baby is okay. I'm relieved to hear it."

"The doctor says everything's fine, but I can tell Paige is concerned about going into early labor again. How could she not be?"

"My sister went through that. It's scary." Benton fiddled with his coffee cup. "I'm glad you were there to support her yesterday."

"I am, too. If something had happened to Peanut—the baby—I don't know what I would've done." Kellan bent forward, elbows on his knees, gaze on the bland rug below.

"Of course. You care about them." Benton's comment felt open ended, but there was a reason. He was good at waiting for Kellan to get to the point, rather than putting words in his mouth.

So Kellan might as well jump in with both feet. "Here's the thing, Benton. Much as I care for Paige—as my friend, okay?"

"Uh-huh." It was hard to tell by Benton's tone whether he believed Kellan or not.

"I'm wrestling with what *care* looks like in this instance. You know she's Drew's sister."

"Yes, and I know his death has been a source of tremendous struggle for you." Benton sounded more like a pastor now than a friend. "Has her being here been a difficult reminder of his death?"

"I've been in more medical offices in the past month than I have in years, and yeah, it triggers some painful memories."

"Of your injury, or Drew?"

His gunshot wound? Hardly. "Drew. But I should add not all the memories are about his death. His life, too. Sometimes she gets a look that reminds me of him, and it's like he's still around for an instant or two. I'm grateful for that. But of course, the way Drew died is still on my mind a lot. How can it not be?" He swallowed down a painful lump. "How can my role in Drew's death not be on my mind all the time? If Paige knew—well, she can't know. It could cause her so much stress she could go into preterm labor again."

"So it sounds like you're grappling with your memories of the past as well as issues in the present. You're wondering how to protect her but struggling with it, because it sounds to me like you actually want to tell her the whole story."

"I almost told her yesterday. She knew something was bothering me and, well, it is. She and her mom don't know what really happened in Afghanistan. They think Drew was killed by insurgents."

"Which is true."

"But Paige and her mom don't know we were on that road because of me."

· Benton leaned forward, mirroring Kellan's pose. "Not out of malice or disobedience or recklessness. You received credible information from a source who'd helped you before. Why wouldn't you trust him again when he offered you intel?"

"I wish I hadn't."

"You did the best you could with the information you had. You were a good, honorable soldier and a good, honorable friend." He leaned back and took a sip of his coffee. "Outside of wanting to protect Paige while her pregnancy is higher risk, is there an official or legal reason why you shouldn't tell Paige and her mom what happened?"

"It's not classified, if that's what you mean. But my superiors advised me to keep my mouth shut for the Faraday family's sake. Not ordered. Advised. Which has left me grappling."

"I can see why. Telling Paige the whole story could bring about repercussions. Big ones, aside from adding to Paige's stress. I'll pray with you about this. But you know, this secret has been hanging over you for four years. Secrets can hold a lot of power over us until they're brought into the light." He almost sounded like he'd lived it, so emphatic was he at that moment.

Kellan scrubbed his face with his hands. "I'm not important in this equation."

"I disagree. So don't you think it's time you come clean with yourself?"

"What do you mean? I'm fully aware of what I did."

"Yes, but you haven't forgiven yourself for something which, frankly, doesn't seem like it's really your fault. Tragedies happen, Kellan, but what happened to Drew is not the end of the story."

"It is for me. My past completely defines me and everything I do."

"Your past *shapes* you, yes, but defines? I thought God was responsible for that role." Benton leaned forward. "Is that how you see Paige? Defined by her past?"

"Of course not."

"So you've extended grace to Paige, but not yourself. What makes you so special? So unique that God can't redeem you, embrace you, change you? Or are you suggesting God's grace and mercy is real enough, strong enough, to extend to everyone except for you?"

He hadn't thought of it that way. He definitely wouldn't view Paige or anyone else in light of their pasts. Except—

"I feel like I'm worse than everyone else, though."

"You're not alone there. Maybe you should read some Apostle Paul when you get home. He called himself the chief of sinners, you'll recall." Benton picked up his bear claw.

"Point taken." Kellan stared at his friend with an expression of mock derision. "I came to you for answers and all you've given me are more questions."

"Sorry." Benton grinned. "But you know

you've got my prayers. And my friendship and my support. I'm here for you. And for Paige. No matter what happens between the two of you."

"Nothing's going to happen. She's leaving town once she figures out where God's leading her."

"Ah, that's right." Benton stretched out his legs. "I'll pray she gets the answers she's looking for, too."

For the millionth time, Kellan despaired at his role in Drew's death. Not just because he was responsible for someone else dying, but because that person's sister was Paige, the one person whose smile and heart touched him like no one else's.

Even though Kellan knew it was impossible, a small part of him couldn't help wishing the divergent paths he and Paige were on weren't leading them to live in different towns. Much as he wanted God to bless her and place her where He wanted her to be, Kellan would sorely miss her when she was out of his life.

Paige entered the bookstore office and found a pastry on a fast-food type napkin on the smaller desk, right beside the computer. Kellan sat behind the larger desk, holding a newspaper. "Good morning, Paige."

"Hi. Did you bring me a bear claw?" Paige picked up the sticky treat that was larger than the palm of her hand. "How'd you know how much I love these?"

"I didn't, but I hoped you didn't hate them or anything. They're one of Angel Food's specialties, along with their raspberry scones. You can't live in Widow's Peak Creek and not have tried one of each."

The buttery pastry melted in her mouth, leaving the thick almond paste on her tongue. Delicious. After she washed it down with a sip of the herbal tea she'd brought in her travel mug, she wiped her sugary fingers on the napkin's edge. "Where's yours?"

"I already had one. I met with Benton this morning." He turned away to switch on his computer.

"I liked him. And your church." She'd initially felt weird about attending, self-conscious of her baby bump, but everyone had been nice. It had felt good to be in fellowship. "I'd like to go again on Sunday."

"Did you want to ride together?"

Was that an invitation? Or was he inquiring about her expectations? "Not if you have plans afterward or something."

"Actually, Gran told me there's some sort of garden party at Creekside Sunday afternoon.

I don't know if Trudie mentioned it to you, but I'm sure she'll invite you. We could go together, if you want."

"It wouldn't be a bad idea. Sure."

"Sounds like a date." His shoulders stiffened. "Not a date. You know what I mean."

"Oh, yeah." She shrugged with perfectly executed nonchalance. She would not read into his slip of the tongue. In fact, she should probably stop thinking about it altogether and start focusing on work. "So you said something about incomplete data entry?"

"And a few other administrative things I've put off, since Don's been pulling my attention toward a second store, but that's another story. Have a seat." As she did, he leaned around her to wake up the computer. As his sleeve brushed hers, an ice-cold jolt shocked her to the shoulder, followed by a trail of goose bumps down her arm.

Get a grip.

He shifted away an inch as if he, too, had been aware of their brief contact and didn't plan to repeat it. "I created files for you this morning, with your name and the topic, so you can find them easily."

"You literally offered me the job last night. You must have stayed up late organizing these for me."

"Early this morning. Anyway, your help with these is a huge blessing." He went through the files, not touching her as he pointed out the files listed on the screen, but that didn't make her any less aware of his proximity. The hair on her forearms stood on end.

But she would be professional and competent. "Which file takes top priority? I'll start there."

"I'd like to ensure that Open Book can fund at least three more book drives through the calendar year, if possible. Little Lambs in the fall, and two holiday drives. Not sure for whom yet, but I want the funds there as God gives us the opportunities. Would you work on this file first, please, so I can have those numbers ready for Don?"

"Of course."

"Great. I'll be out on the shop floor if you have any questions, but don't forget the doctor said to move around."

"I'll come out and say hi to Herb in a while."

Kellan's mouth formed an O. "I forgot to start his coffee. See you later."

Soon, the rich odor of coffee carried from the kitchenette to the office, and she smiled, knowing Herb would be arriving soon. At her break, she'd have to tell him she and the baby were fine. But for now? She'd better get going on this file. She set the timer on her phone for one hour, at which point she'd stretch her legs. Popping her knuckles, she set to work.

It turned out to be more enjoyable than she expected. Sure, she liked being out in the store with customers, but the task was interesting. In the past six months, Kellan—or Open Book, to be precise—had offered several book drives for local nonprofits, with beneficiaries as varied as a school kids' club and a substance abuse rehab facility's library.

All kinds of groups benefited from books, didn't they? She'd never thought about it before. Did Creekside Retirement Village have a library? Could they use something like this?

What about that veterans' group in Pinehurst that Belinda had mentioned to her?

Inspired, she jotted down notes for possible projects. She also noted a few places where the book drives hadn't been as successful. She scrawled down her thoughts. *Needs more publicity to draw awareness to the nonprofit and increase public participation. How? Posters? Invite the media?* She starred that last idea.

She was so engrossed that when her phone alarm went off, she about jumped out of her skin.

"Time to stand up and get the blood flowing, Peanut." Patting her tummy, Paige rose for a quick stretch. She'd finished her herbal tea, and she could use some water. In the kitchenette, she dumped her tea bag, rinsed her travel mug and filled it with filtered water from the fridge.

Now, to visit with Herb. She stepped out from the employee area and came out the door beneath the staircase.

"That was Paige's idea." Kellan's voice caught her attention. What was her idea? She stepped out, but he wasn't there—on the first floor, at least. From her vantage she could see his brown chukka boots descending the staircase from the second floor, followed by a woman wearing green ballet flats. "We're fitting so many more kids up here now."

Paige came around to the foot of the stairs to see who was wearing the green shoes. She recognized the bob-haired woman at once— Faith Latham, who ran the antiques store. "Hi, Faith."

"Paige, there you are. The kids' section looks amazing. That toy display is so cute. Clever use of the armoire, taking the doors off it like that."

"Paige is responsible for all of it. She's been amazing at Open Book." Kellan's smile was soft. "I wish we could keep her here forever, but she has bigger and better plans. Teaching preschool."

"How exciting." Faith pointed up the stairs. "I can already tell you know how to set up a room."

Two dark-haired kids appeared behind her at the top of the stairs, two or three books in each hand. When they saw Paige, the little boy froze in place, but the little girl smiled. Faith beckoned them down. "Logan, Nora, come say hi to Miss Faraday. Paige, these are my favorite kids in the world."

"Miss Faith's going to be our new mommy soon," Nora announced. "I'm going to wear a pretty dress at the wedding and it's green like the chairs in front of the store."

Ah, the sea-foam chairs set outside Faith's antiques store. "You'll look beautiful, I'm sure. And Logan will look quite dashing. Are you wearing a tie for the ceremony?"

"If I have to." Logan absently rubbed his neck.

How old were these kids? Six or seven? They were adorable. It was both weird and wonderful to think that someday, Peanut would be their size, reading books, wiggling loose teeth like the little boy was now doing, chattering like the girl about her dress. Boy or girl, Paige didn't care. She just couldn't wait to meet Peanut.

"I'd better drop in on Herb, but you guys

enjoy those books." She smiled at the kids and Faith.

Kellan wasn't looking at her, though. His concerned gaze fixed over Paige's shoulder.

Paige spun. A willowy woman with cropped dark hair approached the staircase, and Paige's stomach fell to her soles. What was her mother doing here?

Mom saw her then, and before Paige could greet her, she bustled forward. "Hi, honey. I thought I'd surprise you for a long weekend."

It was a surprise, all right. For both of them, because her mother's gaze fell to Paige's six-months-pregnant stomach and her smile dissolved into a scowl.

Despite Paige's best intentions not to disappoint her mom, she'd completely, utterly failed.

Chapter Fifteen

Paige's throat filled with—what was the name for this ache? Regret? Sorrow? A sense of justification? She'd known Mom would be disappointed.

In her peripheral vision, she caught sight of Faith and the kids silently making their way to the checkout counter. Kellan's face was grief stricken, but he forced a smile. "Why don't you take the day, Paige?" His voice was gentle. "Those files can sit awhile longer."

How kind he was, giving her time to talk to her mother. "Thanks, Kellan."

"Nonsense." Mom's tone was bright, but her cheeks mottled, like she was either enraged or about to cry. "I'll meet you at your place after your shift, all right? Gives me time to do a few things around town."

What things? Mom was clearly making up an excuse.

She'd give her mom all the time she needed, though. "I'll be there at ten after five."

"You can leave early, anyway, if you want," Kellan offered, quiet, his voice for her alone. "The stress—"

"I'm fine." Mom turned on her heel and left the store, and Paige returned to the office without visiting Herb. Her fingers shook as she took hold of the computer mouse. It would be a long day.

But it ended eventually, and Paige arrived at her tiny house before her mom did, giving her just enough time to tidy up the textbooks and homework materials she'd left out on the love seat before her mother knocked on the door.

Paige welcomed her inside, arm extended for a hug, but Mom walked right past. All right, then. Paige shut the door behind her. "Would you like something to drink?"

"Water, please." Mom perched on the edge of the love seat and looked around with narrowed eyes. "This is cozy."

The way Mom said it, Paige wasn't sure if she meant that as a good or bad thing. She poured them both glasses of ice water. "It's been perfect for what I needed." She sat on the narrow recliner, praying for the right words.

She might as well start with the thing that had been weighing on her most heavily.

"This isn't how I wanted you to find out about the baby."

"Were you ever going to tell me?" Mom set down her glass without taking a drink. "Was everything you told me last month a lie?"

"No, it was all true. I lacked meaningful work in San Jose, spring semester ended, Aidan dumped me and had me evicted. So I decided to come to Widow's Peak Creek."

"To take time for yourself, you said. To regroup. You just didn't mention anything about having a baby." Mom glanced at Paige's stomach, her eyes full of sorrow. "Is it because you're giving the baby up for adoption? That's why you didn't tell me?"

"No, Mom. I'm keeping the baby." Her hand went protectively to her stomach. "And I'll be raising him or her by myself. Aidan… Aidan won't be involved. He signed away his parental rights. He doesn't want anything to do with us."

Mom mumbled an uncharitable name for Aidan. "I still don't understand why you didn't say anything to me."

"I wanted to have a plan in place first. It's always been so important to you that I stand on my own two feet. I didn't want you to think

I expected anything from you, so my intention was to have everything worked out before I told you. Unfortunately, I'm not there yet." She stared at her fingernails. "I guess Aunt Trudie called you when I went into early labor?"

"What?" Mom squawked like a parrot. "You went into labor? Are you okay?"

"I'm fine—I assumed that's why you're here."

"I wish Trudie had called me. No, that's not true. I wish *you* had called me. I wish you hadn't told my aunt before you told your own mother."

It ached that her mom sounded so angry. Paige couldn't blame her, though. "I'm sorry, Mom. You're right. I should've told you."

Mom still looked hurt, but she shrugged. "Preterm labor, honey? That's horrible."

"It was scary, but I have a great doctor, and she said it was probably a onetime thing, so I don't need to stay confined to bed. She does want me to take things easier, though, so Kellan offered me administrative work so I'm not on my feet all day."

"How accommodating of him. You said in your text that this is his house, too?" Mom sounded disapproving.

Paige tried not to read into her mom's tone. "His and Marigold's. His neighbor on that side." She pointed in the direction of Marigold's house. "It straddles their property line. She's a lovely woman, friends with Aunt Trudie and Kellan's grandma." None of that was important right now, though. "So if Trudie didn't call you, why did you come?"

Mom traced her buffed nail over the lip of her glass. "I wanted to visit. See my daughter." Mom squared her shoulders. "You said a moment ago that you don't know what to do next, is that correct?"

"Not yet, no." She shouldn't feel this ashamed, but heat rushed up her chest to her neck. "I'm taking online courses to finish up school. But as to where to go? I'm still praying about that."

"Well, it sounds like you need to do more than pray. You've had a month to figure this out already." Mom pulled her cell phone out from her purse. "It's good I came when I did, because we have a lot to do."

"To prepare for the baby, you mean?"

"That, and to get you situated in Sacramento. You're coming home with me. Tomorrow."

Paige clutched her glass. "I'm not leaving, Mom."

Mom looked up from typing into her phone. "What's keeping you here? Your classes are online, you said. Your job does nothing toward reaching your goal of teaching preschool. There's nothing for you here."

It was almost funny, how the imaginary voice of her mother that she heard in her head sometimes was right here, come to life, in her tiny house. "Right or wrong of me, this is why I hadn't told you yet. You raised me to look out for myself, and I'm doing that. I'm working out a plan that you can't find fault with."

"I'm finding a lot of fault with this whole situation, Paige. I taught you to get your ducks in a row. To pay your own way. To know how to take care of yourself. But look at you. You put your faith in a man and now you're unmarried, pregnant and still not teaching preschool like you've always wanted." Mom ticked the shortcomings off on her fingers. "You knew how hard life was for me when I was in your position, how long it took me to pay off debt and build the foundation for my realty business, but clearly you didn't heed the warning of my example, because here you are."

Hurt and shame rushed through Paige, along with anger. But she wouldn't raise her voice. "I love you, Mom, and you deserved better than me not telling you about the baby. I'm sorry for that, and for the things you've missed like news of the baby's first kick and hearing about my weird craving for pickles. But my goals haven't changed. I'm still going to teach preschool. Yes, people like Kellan have helped me, but I'm paying my way. And I trust God will work out my future. I'm not going home with you tomorrow."

Before her mom could respond, Paige lifted her hand. "You came for a visit, and I'd still like us to have one. Stay, like you planned. You can sleep in my bed upstairs, and I'll take the recliner, or you can stay at one of the inns in town, if you'd be more comfortable. There are several lovely places along the creek."

"You're not hearing me, Paige."

"Yes, I am, but we're at an impasse, so I'd prefer to talk about our weekend together. Tomorrow we can shop along historic Main Street, go out to lunch, whatever you like. Sunday I'm going to church, and I'd love for you to join me. Afterward, there's a garden party at Creekside Retirement Village, and I'm sure Aunt Trudie would love for you to come. You can meet Marigold and Eileen Lambert, Kellan's grandma."

Mom stared at her with her mouth open. Then it clamped shut. "You'll move back home with me. I'm going to take the weekend to prove it to you."

That didn't sound remotely enjoyable, but

Paige smiled, anyway. "How about I put together a light dinner for us? Does chef salad sound good?"

"Actually, yes." Mom's mulish expression softened a fraction. "You do that while I respond to a few work texts, if you don't mind."

Paige didn't normally put pickles on her chef salad, but she would tonight. She needed a treat after Mom's harsh words. She got busy boiling two eggs and preparing vegetables. Washing the lettuce, her gaze lifted.

Kellan stood out in his backyard, tossing balls to the dogs, darting glances in her direction. Could he see through her window? There was enough distance between her kitchen and his yard, maybe all he could see in her window was a reflection. Or possibly her silhouette.

Little Sydney lumbered toward him, her short corgi legs hardly longer than the blades of grass. Kellan crouched to play with her, grabbing a rope for them to play tug-of-war. Paige couldn't help but smile, despite the tension in her house.

A longing seized her, for him to look up at her window and see her. For him to wave— no, for him to knock on the door of her tiny house and come inside. She liked being with him. Felt calmer, happier, when he was near.

Chopping turkey, she realized it was time to

admit to herself what she'd been fighting for a while now. She wasn't just attracted to him. She was in danger of falling in love with him. Even though he was as firm in his decision to be single as she was. Even though she was pregnant with another man's baby.

Even though there was no way it would ever work out between them, she realized a part of her wished it could.

"What's out there?" Mom stood up to join her at the sink.

"Kellan and the dogs." Thankfully, her voice didn't tremble. But she flipped her hair over her shoulder to hide her face from her mother, so she wouldn't see her blush.

Kellan hadn't relaxed all weekend. He'd sneaked glances at the tiny house Thursday evening when he was out with the dogs, curious about what was going on with Paige and her mom. He'd finally sent her a quick text that night to ask about church, but the truth was, he needed to know Paige was okay. His stomach ached with worry for her.

She'd filled him in on her mom's plan to take her to Sacramento. *Unmarried, pregnant, not teaching.* Harsh words that must have pained Paige to hear. Paige hadn't exaggerated when she'd said her mom would be unhappy with her.

He'd seethed at her mom, tried to encourage Paige over text, offered to come over, but she'd held him off. She'd also promised she had no intentions of leaving town yet. I can't quit Open Book now. I promised my boss I'd get through a pile of data entry, she'd jokingly texted.

Every evening since, they checked in via text. Light, nothing intense. Just enough that he knew she was all right. Enough to send him to sleep with a smile each evening.

But he was tense again on Sunday afternoon on the grassy lawn at Creekside for the garden party, watching Paige and her mom stroll to the dessert table. He certainly wasn't making conversation with the three ladies seated with him on the stone benches near the bocce court, so it was no surprise Gran nudged him in the arm with her shoulder. "You're glowering at them, sweetheart."

"I just hope this visit isn't too hard on Paige. She's supposed to avoid stress."

"She seems all right," Gran said. "Healthy and pretty in that dress."

The long dress, striped in mustard, black and green, did flatter her, but that didn't mean she wasn't anxious. He'd noticed the tight set of her mouth during church this morning, and

she'd barely picked at her chicken salad crois-
sant at lunch.

Trudie clucked her tongue. "Joyce read me
the riot act for not telling her Paige was pregnant. I may not have agreed with Paige's choice
to keep it from her, but I better understand it
now. If it's so important to Joyce that Paige
be independent, then why is she fighting her
about staying here? Why does she want her to
live with her in Sacramento?"

"Maybe because there's a baby involved,"
Marigold mused. "Joyce lost her son and she
doesn't want to lose her daughter and grand-
child now, too."

Despite the heat of the afternoon, Kellan's
skin chilled. Everything happening right now
was traceable back to Afghanistan, wasn't it?
All of it started with him—

"Time to execute plan B, ladies," Marigold
said.

"Agreed," Gran said. Trudie nodded.

Kellan's already writhing stomach seemed to
sink deeper into his abdomen. "What's plan B?"

"It was supposed to be secret, but the matter has reached now-or-never status, so we're
going to have to fill you in, Kellan." Marigold
stood.

Kellan stood, too. "Please tell me you're not
playing matchmaker for me and Paige again."

Gran gaped. "He figured it out."

"Of course Paige and I figured it out. That bocce thing was pretty obvious. So was the cake table ploy."

"Now you get to be in on it, too." Trudie clapped. "We need to get you and Paige alone so you can ensure she's not caving in to her mom's pressure to leave. When she and Joyce come back, I'll ask Joyce to help me change my email settings. She'll have no choice but to come inside with me."

"No, don't do all of that. Please." A pit in Kellan's stomach burned.

Marigold's smile fell. "Don't you want Paige to stay in town?"

"Of course I do." He was so angry and grieved at the thought of her leaving, his hands fisted. "But she's always been up-front about her intention to leave town. I'll support Paige in whatever decision she makes about the timing, but she has to be the one to make it. She doesn't need me, or us, to interfere."

"It's not interfering. It's helping." Gran batted her lashes.

"And you, my dear boy, need help, too, before you get her away." Marigold's look was stern.

They had no idea how difficult this moment was for him. The secret of Drew's death had

been smoldering inside him so long he'd figured out how to brush it aside and pretend like
everything was fine. He couldn't pretend anymore, though. Right now it felt as if his secret
burned a hole through his stomach. "There's
nothing between us, ladies. I'm sorry, but her
life is complicated. And so is mine."

Gran touched his arm. "Complications have
a way of smoothing out. It's obvious to the
three of us that you are in love with that young
woman."

"No." He couldn't be. He'd fought against it
harder than he'd ever fought anything.

"And she's in love with you."

"She's not. She doesn't want to be with anyone."

"Then why is she staring at you?"

He looked up and met Paige's curious gaze.

"You're going to keep lying to us? To yourself?" Marigold cupped his cheek, drawing
him around so his back was to Paige. "Poor
boy."

He was not the one to be pitied here. Not
when he was responsible for Drew's death.
"What I feel doesn't matter one iota. Paige and
me—it's impossible."

"Why, sweetheart?" Gran's brow furrowed.
"Don't tell me it's the baby."

They weren't going to give up, were they?

The secret burning a hole through his abdomen seemed to crawl up his throat, as if hoping for release. Swallowing didn't push it all the way down, either.

"Of course it's not the baby. It's me, and if Paige knew what I've done, she'd hate me."

"What did you do?" The feminine voice behind him pierced him like a knife in the gut. He hadn't realized she'd approached while his back was to her.

He turned around and met her wary gaze. And his heart sank to his shoes.

He'd despaired of this moment for four years. He'd agonized over what would happen if Paige and her mom learned how Drew died. He hadn't wanted to cause them pain, nor had he wanted to endanger Peanut if Paige experienced more stress.

But it was unavoidable now. The time had come, for good or ill. He wouldn't lie to them. All he could do was pray and trust God to hold the Faradays in His arms while Kellan broke their hearts.

"I'm sorry. To both of you." He included Joyce in his apology. "I don't want to cause you any stress, Paige, but I've been holding something back from you. Maybe we should go somewhere more private."

"Tell me here, now." Paige's gaze never wavered from his.

So he stared into her eyes, his heart breaking down the middle, praying his words wouldn't cause her to go into early labor again.

"Drew's death didn't happen quite like you were told. The truth is, I'm responsible for what happened in Afghanistan. He's dead because of me."

Chapter Sixteen

He'd lied to her. Paige knew in the deepest recesses of her being that he wasn't lying now, though, the way sorrow faded his blue eyes to gray.

All this time, he'd lied to her.

"Let's go to my condo where we can have privacy." Trudie took Paige's arm, and Paige didn't fight against the support.

They marched silently over the grass to the condos, and within a few minutes Paige was perched on the edge of Trudie's beige couch, gripping her mom's hand. Trudie sat on her other side, wrapping her arm around Paige's shoulders. "Surely, that isn't right, Kellan. Drew was shot by combatants. You're not responsible."

"I am." Kellan paced behind the chairs where Marigold and Eileen sat, his movements like that of a caged tiger—agitated, tense, holding back a powerful desire to bolt or break something.

Paige couldn't muster an ounce of empathy for the agony he was going through, though. Not if he was at fault for Drew's death.

"Outside our base camp, I'd become acquainted with a local guy—hardly more than a kid. We talked bicycles. I helped him patch a tire. Others told me he was a reliable source when it came to intel on the safest routes, stuff like that, so on one occasion I asked him for insight on which road to take. His information spared us from an IED. So on another occasion when he warned me to take one route over another, I believed him. But it turned out I'd offended him when I assisted some other guy with his bike chain. A guy he didn't like. So he lied to me and set us up."

Paige's intake of breath lodged somewhere around her breastbone. She was aware of Mom's sudden clutch on her hand, Marigold's gasp, Trudie's stiffening posture, but she couldn't tear her gaze away from Kellan.

"It was a trap." Kellan stopped pacing and scrubbed the back of his neck with his hands. "There was a landslide blocking the road. I had guard duty while the others figured out whether it was safe to go around. I didn't see a single sign of warning. If I had—but I didn't, and Drew came to spell me. He sent me back to the Humvee for a piece of equipment. I hadn't taken two steps when—when he was shot. It was supposed to be me, not him."

His eyes clouded, as if he was seeing the firefight all over again.

So this was what he'd been going through. All that time, she'd sensed his pain, noticed his face losing expression, suspected a wound. She'd known he kept something from her. Something he wasn't ready to talk about.

Never in a million years did Paige think it was this.

Eileen stood and wrapped her arms around his waist. "No, darling, it was an accident. You were shot, too. And since then, survivor's guilt has been eating you alive, hasn't it?"

Survivor's guilt. Tears stung Paige's eyes. She took a tissue from Aunt Trudie and blotted her eyes. She wanted them clear for the remainder of this conversation.

"I went to him," Kellan continued. "Promised him I'd make it up to him. Prayed with him. I don't know if he heard me, but I was with him."

"Why didn't the army tell us any of this?" Mom's voice shook. "Why didn't *you*? You were in our home. At Drew's funeral. You and

Paige have caught up a few times since then, and for a month now, she's been yards from your house, working in your store. You had numerous opportunities to say something. Why didn't you?"

"I was instructed to keep quiet. Every one of my superiors, as well as the counselors I spoke to, said the details would cause your family more harm than help. But I've wrestled every day since, wanting to tell you everything, and at the same time wanting to protect you."

"Protect." Paige stuffed the damp tissue in her dress pocket. "Interesting choice of words, Kellan, because the only person you've protected is yourself."

"I deserve that, but this was no light decision, Paige."

"I heard what you said out there in the yard. That if I knew what you'd done, I'd hate you. Well, *hate* is a strong word, but everything's different now. I don't know which is worse, that you trusted the wrong person and it cost me my brother, or that you've been lying to me this whole time."

"Paige." Aunt Trudie's voice was soft. "Kellan isn't a liar."

"Isn't he?" As Paige stood, her brain filled with snippets of memories from the past four weeks. Happy memories, now tainted. "The whole reason you helped me is because you feel guilt over Drew, isn't it?"

"I did promise him I'd help you however I could, yes."

"The job, the tiny house and your so-called friendship were ways to assuage your guilt."

"Guilt played a role, but I truly care about you, Paige." His eyes bored into hers, pleading. "Your friendship matters to me more than you know."

"How could I ever believe that? You didn't need an employee at Open Book, did you? You lied to me about that, surely."

And right now she was as angry with herself as she was with him. She'd known better than to trust a man again. Yet, she'd allowed her heart and mind to get muddled by Kellan's smile and kindness and generosity. It had only been a few days since she'd stood in her kitchen and admitted she had started to develop feelings for him. Real feelings.

His betrayal hurt worse than preterm labor had.

She straightened her shoulders. "Marigold, I'll leave my last month's rent payment on the kitchen table with my key."

"You're leaving? No, Paige." Marigold wiped her damp cheeks. "Let's talk this through."

"Thank you, but I'm going to accept my mom's invitation to stay with her for a while. If it's still okay, Mom?"

"Absolutely." Mom stood with her.

Paige's motto about the blue sky behind the dark clouds? Clearly, her blue sky was not in Widow's Peak Creek, after all.

Aunt Trudie's chin trembled. "But Drew's death was an accident, Paige. Kellan didn't cause it."

Right now she wasn't so sure how she felt about that particular part of the conversation. But she knew precisely how she felt about Kellan. She glared at him, hoping he'd hear every word. "It's not that. I'm upset that you lied. Knowing how I'd been hurt by a liar. Knowing I made that choice to protect my baby. Maybe you thought I wouldn't be here long so it wouldn't matter—"

"That's not what I thought."

"It doesn't matter, though. You knew things about me. You and I were close." She couldn't say any more than that, couldn't admit to him that she'd actually been stupid enough to be close to falling in love with him.

"All this time, you were betraying me." She ignored the pain in his eyes. "I never want to see you again."

Despite the complicated emotions at war in his chest, despite the screams of his heart to ask her to stay and talk, Kellan respected Paige's wishes. He didn't chase after her.

Nor did he visit the tiny house later on, although he saw enough foot traffic in the driveway between his house and Marigold's to know that several people, including Gran and even Mickey, had come to see her Sunday evening.

When he took the dogs into the yard to play, Marigold set down her pruning shears and left the roses, speed walking to him. "Oh, Kellan."

"I'm sorry, Marigold."

"I'm the one who's sorry. You two care about each other. This shouldn't be happening."

He held up a hand, even as he kept one eye on Sydney while the pup explored the crevice between the gate and the fence. "It's for the best."

Hard as this was, he couldn't deny that there was a sense of peace now that the truth had come out. But that didn't mean he was happy. Hardly. Better able to heal, maybe, but a long way from happy.

Marigold sighed. "We've convinced her she can't leave until we've thrown her a baby shower. It's on Tuesday and it's in the kids' section of the bookstore, because she should be able to enjoy that space one last time."

"Who's *we*?"

"Me. And everyone else. She made that place

special, and there are a lot of people who want to give her and that baby a proper send-off."

"I know she doesn't want to see me. I have to be at Open Book Tuesday, but I'll stay in the office. I'd like to talk to her mom, though, if I can."

"I'll pray for the opportunity for you, Kellan dear."

Kellan prayed, too, and when Tuesday came, he smiled at Gran, Marigold and Trudie as they carried blue-and-pink balloons, Tupperware containers and tote bags upstairs. He offered to help but they'd turned him away with sorrowful eyes, like they didn't want him to see what he'd be missing.

"I'll save you some cake, honey." Gran patted his cheek.

"Thanks." But he didn't think he'd be able to eat it.

He worked the bookstore floor until it neared one o'clock, the hour of his scheduled phone call with a distributor, as well as the time of the baby shower. As he chatted with the distributor, snippets of laughter and conversation carried through the office door. Guests must be arriving. He focused as best he could on the business at hand, even if his mind wandered upstairs. Paige was here, so close. But so far away.

Soon after his short conversation ended, a knock rapped on the door. One of his part-time employees worked the register, but if he'd needed help, he would have used the intercom on the phone, so maybe it was one of the shower guests. His posture straightened. "Come in."

Benton poked his head in the door. "Bad time?"

"Never. Here for the party?"

"Yup, but I thought I'd say hi first." He shut the door behind him and sat behind the desk Paige used for a short time. He set down a greeting card envelope and flicked lint from the sleeve of his dress shirt in a nervous gesture. "As a pastor, I've attended all sorts of events, from middle school musicals to a quinceañera, but this is my first baby shower."

"I've never been to one, either, but you won't be the only man. Herb was invited."

"I heard your grandma baked her famous cake. That's enough to entice me." He rubbed his flat stomach. "Are you sure you don't want to come up with me?"

"If I run up there, it won't be for cake. It'll be to drop off a present. She doesn't want me there." No need to explain the *she* meant Paige. "Maybe it was wrong of me to get a present for the baby. I couldn't help it, though."

It had been difficult to stop at just one gift. He wanted to buy Peanut everything he or she would ever need. He couldn't, of course, but he boxed up the books on pregnancy that he'd ordered. No need to read those now. He'd make sure Paige got them somehow, though.

"You miss her already, don't you?"

"I do." Her laugh. Her sunshine. "I know I'll live, though. Just like I've been living every day since Drew died, trying to make his death up to him. To God. The world. Paige."

"*Living* isn't the word I'd choose. I'd say surviving. Breathing and functioning, but you're not living into the freedom and peace God has for you."

"So what do I do? Pray more?"

"Praying never hurts, but what do you think you should do?"

He leaned back in his chair and his eye caught something on the table beside Benton. Paige's handwriting. "Hand me that, will you?"

Benton gave it to him, his expression patient but interested.

It was a list from her last day of work here. Kellan read it twice.

Speak to Kellan about his planned book drives. But for which nonprofits? Creekside Retirement Village? What about the Veterans' Group in Pinehurst? Could be coordinated

with Veterans' Day to honor local veterans.
Give back to those who gave so much for us.

"What is it?" Benton leaned forward.

"Her last day here, Paige was working on numbers for future book drives. Looks like she had some ideas, including a drive for the veterans' group in Pinehurst. She has no way of knowing, but my mom told me their library is pretty bare. They deserve better than that. They should receive as much honor as we can give them."

"You're right, both of you."

Kellan tapped his thumb on the desktop. "Both my mother and the army counselor suggested I join a veterans' group to talk about the night Drew died. Obviously, I haven't. I'm afraid they won't understand what happened. I don't want to take away from anyone there struggling with a real need, either."

Benton scratched the stubble on his jaw. "I hear that a lot. 'Other people have it worse than me.' 'My need isn't as significant as someone else's.' Well, the truth is, everyone needs for someone to listen to them from time to time. My belief is that God can heal us instantaneously, with a touch or a word, but sometimes His plan seems to be to heal over time, through a process in which we have to lean on Him and allow others to lift us up." He stretched out his legs. "I can relate to you as a brother and friend, but no one will understand your experience as well as someone who's actually been there the way you have. In those boots, in that desert. The secret is out, Kellan. Might as well give that group a try. You could help someone, and who knows? You might be helped, too, and forgive yourself, once and for all."

"Yeah, the idea of forgiving myself has not been foremost in my mind since we last talked."

"I think your inability to forgive yourself has affected you more than you realize. Could it be why you resist Don's push to expand to a second location?"

"It was never my focus. Besides, I don't want to be spread too thin."

"If anyone can handle two stores, it's you. Two stores could mean double the blessings like book drives, you know. If you're spending some time in Pinehurst for the veterans' group, anyway, it's not that big of a hardship."

Surely, Don hadn't planned it this way, but the vacant building he'd selected for the second bookstore was literally steps from the veterans' center on the same tree-lined street.

"I'm praying, Kellan. For Paige, too. I want you both to have peace." Benton stood, scooping up the envelope he'd brought. "I should probably get upstairs. Are you sure you don't want to come with me?"

"It's better if I sneak in and out. My friendship with Paige is irretrievably broken."

"Friendship." Benton snorted. "I know it's more than that, but whatever you say."

Kellan walked out with him, bringing him face-to-face with Joyce Faraday as she prepared to mount the stairs to the baby shower.

Joyce's smile was tight. "Hello."

Benton extended his hand. "Good to see you again, Mrs. Faraday."

"Yes. You're the preacher." She looked abashed. "I don't go to church, but Paige holds you in high regard."

"It's mutual. She's been a wonderful addition to our little town." Benton gestured to the staircase. "Heading upstairs to the party?"

Kellan held up a hand. "Before you go, Joyce, I wondered if there is a good time to talk before you and Paige leave town."

Her dark-eyed gaze reminded him so much of Drew it made his gut ache. "I'd actually hoped to talk to you, too. I can spare a minute now."

Kellan would take that minute. Whatever Joyce wanted—to yell at him, or ask questions, or threaten him with a lawsuit—he didn't care. God had given them an opening to talk, a chance for him to apologize.

He owed her that, and so much more.

Chapter Seventeen

A pile of opened presents mounded atop the metal folding chair beside Paige, all things she would put to good use once Peanut arrived. A yellow duckie towel and matching washcloths. Footed pajamas decorated with orange elephants. An antique silver spoon from Faith, along with a modern set of bibs and burp cloths. A giraffe teether from Jane. A gift card from Benton, and cardboard baby books from Mickey and Herb, who sat front and center in the group of chairs.

"Mickey told me that caterpillar book was a good choice." He clamped his mouth shut the moment the words were out, as if he feared he'd said too much.

A rush of fondness for him poured over Paige. "It's perfect. The baby will love it."

But Paige loved it, too, and all of the other

gifts, because each item would not only bless her and the baby but would also serve as a re-minder of the gift-giver. These people gath-ered here had touched her life in a profound and meaningful way.

Paige scanned the room, memorizing the guests' faces as they chatted amongst them-selves. She'd only been in Widow's Peak Creek for a month, but already her heart ached at the thought of not seeing these people again for a while. Marigold, Eileen and Aunt Trudie, chat-ting with Benton. The bookstore gang, like Mickey and Herb. Faith and Jane. A few of the parents from Toddler Story Time. Tanya, the social director from Creekside. Even Kel-lan's mom, Belinda, had come, but not Don. He visited one of the other in-town businesses he'd invested in. Nevertheless, she was sur-rounded by many more people than she'd ex-pected, after such a short acquaintance.

Mom, though, wasn't even here. She was late—hopefully nothing was wrong, like a flat tire—but her mother's imaginary voice whis-pered in her ear. These people hardly knew her. They'd only come because they pitied her. Paige's heart sank to her stomach.

That voice that sounded so much like Mom wasn't real, though, was it? No matter why these folks had come today, their intention was to bless her and Peanut. Those attacks in Paige's ear came from inside Paige. And it was time to stop them.

She straightened her spine. "May I have your attention, please? I appreciate you coming on such short notice. Thank you all for your generosity and kindness toward me and Peanut—the baby." Her hand went to her tummy as several people chuckled. "You've all given me so much, and I don't just mean these beautiful gifts."

"It goes both ways." Jane's voice carried through the crowd. "You've been a huge help to Little Lambs."

Paige shook her head. "I came and read one time, that's all."

Tanya scoffed. "You arranged the book buddy program between Creekside and Little Lambs, which we're going to continue."

"It's been great for the kids," Jane said.

"It's fun for our residents, too." Tanya winked at Eileen and Aunt Trudie.

Faith's hand fluttered. "I appreciate you opening up the museum display area and encouraging Kellan to move the relevant kids' books downstairs. Thanks to you, more kids know about history now."

"Open Book has always been great, but you've done wonders up here." One of the moms from Toddler Story Time gestured at the red armoire.

"You helped Kellan, a lot." Belinda had tears in her eyes.

"I don't know about that." Paige stared at the armoire. She didn't want to think about Kellan.

"I do." Marigold's tone wasn't unfriendly, but it brooked no argument. "You've been a blessing to Widow's Peak Creek, my dear, and you'll be missed."

Was that true? She'd spent so much time thinking about how she'd been blessed here, the recipient of so many helping hands, she'd never given a moment's thought to the notion that she'd done anything helpful or good.

Kellan may have lied to her, but he'd said something to her right when she arrived in town. God intended for His children to bear one another's burdens.

Looking back, Paige could see how God had been teaching her that for several months now. Even when she was waiting for Aidan to come back to her, she'd been drawn to church. That was when she first realized that despite her best efforts to live a good life, she couldn't save herself. She needed a Savior for that. Since the day she accepted Jesus, her path had taken her into places where she had to come to terms with needing help. God's. Others'.

And it wasn't the end of the world. In fact, it was a new beginning. She viewed herself differently. She viewed others differently, too. Receiving made her want to reach out with a helping hand to others. She hadn't realized what she was doing at the time, but she'd been part of a chain, in a way, giving and receiving help.

Which meant it wasn't so bad, after all, that she hadn't shouldered all of her troubles alone. Because maybe she wasn't supposed to in the first place.

The realization brought hot, stinging tears to her eyes.

"Aww, we'll miss you, too." Mickey rushed to hug her, misinterpreting her tears, which was fine by Paige.

The *clip-clop* of high heels on the staircase drew her gaze, and there was Mom, arriving at last. "Sorry I'm late. Looks like a nice party." Her gaze took in the pink-and-blue balloons, the refreshment table and the pile of gifts.

Paige slipped from Mickey's hug. "It was. What happened? Did you have car trouble?"

"No, I got caught talking is all. Introduce me to your friends."

Talking to whom? She'd have to ask later. Now she took her mom around the room. They'd spoken to roughly half of the guests when Eileen brandished a long knife. "Texas sheet cake? My specialty."

Without a word, Herb bustled to the refreshment table.

"Paige?" Jane came alongside as others followed Herb for the cake. "I wish you weren't leaving town. One of our aides is going half-time so she can homeschool her kids. You were the first person I thought of to offer the other half of her job to, three hours a day. That would leave you enough free time to work on your courses. And work here, too, if you wanted. It seemed like it would've been a good fit."

Paige's breath caught. Three hours a day? That would have been ideal, since she wasn't supposed to be on her feet all day but neither was she supposed to lie around.

With a yearning so strong it almost made her weak in the knees, she wanted that job, working with Jane and the other sweet ladies at Little Lambs, among the adorable kids.

But how could she stay in a town where Kellan lived? Seeing him would remind her of his lies, and even now her chest ached at the prospect.

Worse, if she saw him around town, she'd never get over him. Because the truth of it was, she'd fallen for him, despite her best attempts not to. With God's help, she'd be able to forgive him eventually, but that didn't mean she could forget that his friendship had been nothing more than his attempt to ease a guilty conscience.

Mom met her before she could join in another conversation, leaning in to speak quietly. "Before we leave Open Book, you should talk to Kellan."

"I don't think so."

"You have a lot to say to one another." Mom's smile was tentative. Encouraging. Not the least bit upset, angry or disapproving.

Paige's head swam with confusion, but that didn't mean she wanted to see Kellan. "I don't have anything else to say to him, actually."

"Then maybe you should listen to him. One last time. I'm late to the party because I got a call back from someone in the army. Kellan was investigated at his own insistence. And cleared. The army holds him blameless, and even though I didn't feel this way at first, now I do, too. I told him as much, downstairs."

"You've talked to him?"

"I did. And you should, too."

Paige faced the wall so the guests wouldn't see her grimace. "His role in Drew's death is not what eats at me, though, Mom. He lied about it. And then he felt so guilty about it that he pretended to be my friend."

"I don't know that young man well, but I sincerely doubt he was ever pretending about that. He's heartsick." Mom dipped her head to look Paige square in the eyes. "He's so crazy about you he's torn up inside. Not that he said so, but it's obvious that man is lovelorn—"

"Paige? Here's your cake." Eileen approached with a plate of her famous creation.

"Thanks," she mumbled. Eileen's cake might be delicious, but Paige had no appetite anymore.

Especially when she caught sight of Kellan lingering at the top of the stairs, a small rectangle in hand. A baby Bible, because even though he'd stuck a bow on top, it wasn't wrapped.

He smiled. "Just wanted to drop this off."

"How thoughtful, Kellan," Jane was saying, but Paige's ears began to buzz.

He looked different, his eyes rimmed with fatigue, his hair ruffled, like he'd been running his hands through it. Like he was genuinely upset.

But his care for her had been fake. That sad expression in his eyes wasn't grief at loss of their friendship; it was remorse for what happened to Drew. And for lying about it until he got caught. Kellan may have felt a connection to her, but beyond that, his kindness had been contrived. That made him no better than Peanut's dad, in her book.

Except—

A cramping spasm of pain wrenched her gut. Her cake fell to the floor with a splat.

"Pain? Preterm labor again?" Mom sounded frantic.

Gritting her teeth from the cramp, Paige could only nod once.

"We need to get you to the doctor's." Mom's voice was loud in Paige's ear.

She shook her head. "The doctor said to go straight to the hospital if I had preterm labor again."

Kellan was at her elbow. "Can you walk down the stairs?"

Could she? She'd try, but those weren't the words that came out. "I don't know."

"I'm the last person you want around, but I'm going to carry you downstairs. You never have to see me again once I get you to the hospital. Okay?"

Even now, after everything they'd been through, he was waiting for her permission. Demonstrating respect for her wishes. As she met his gaze, there was nothing in his eyes but a resolute determination.

Mom was right. They had a hundred things

left to say to one another, but all she could get out through the pain was one word. "Okay."

He swept her into his strong arms. And even though she would probably regret it later, she leaned into his chest, grateful for his help. Because right now it was obvious. She couldn't do this alone.

Kellan tore out of the parking lot and double parked in front of Open Book. Ignoring the horn honking behind him, he flicked on his hazard lights, burst out of the cab and assisted Paige into the back seat. Her mom climbed in after her.

"We'll follow in my car," Marigold shouted.

Kellan could only wave an acknowledgment at her, Gran and Trudie before climbing back behind the wheel. He had to get moving. "We'll be there in a few minutes, Paige."

"Where's the hospital?" Joyce's voice cracked. In the rearview mirror, he could see her soothing Paige's brow with her fingers.

"Not far." Except that the traffic lights weren't cooperating. Nothing he could do but pray, so he did. Out loud. For Paige. For Peanut. For the light to turn green anytime now.

When it did, he floored it. And changed lanes. Twice.

"Kellan?" Paige's voice was low. Strained, yet, but not broken with pain.

"I swerved too hard, didn't I? Sorry. I'll drive more smoothly the rest of the way."

"No, I wanted to thank you for driving me."

"Don't thank me. I'm the one who keeps causing you to go into preterm labor and I'm so sorry, Paige."

"That's not true. You shouldn't feel responsible for any of this."

"I don't just feel responsible, Paige. I am responsible. But more than anything, I want you and Peanut to be all right. I know you don't think I'm trustworthy—"

"Stop."

"Stop the car?" Heart in his throat, he checked his side mirrors to see if he could make a quick lane change. "Do you need to get out?"

"Stop talking. Just for a second. Please. I need to say something."

Joyce's gaze met Kellan's in the rearview mirror. "Go ahead, Paige," she said. "We're listening."

"Mom told me what the army said about Drew's death. I'm glad for the information, not just for our sake, but yours. It was an awful accident, Kellan, and I don't blame you for it. What cut me to the bone was the lying. Because that's what Aidan did to me. And you knew that."

She was right. He'd wounded her in an area that was already scarred.

"But right before I dropped the cake," she continued, "I saw something in your eyes. In you, that reminded me you are nothing like Aidan. You proved that to me time and again. Times that might have been insignificant, but they meant a lot to me, because they revealed your heart. Like providing coffee for Herb. Opening your home to animals. You even asked if you could carry me downstairs rather than just throwing me over your shoulder like a caveman. You've been honoring your promise to my brother. You kept a secret from me, yes, but your care and concern for me weren't lies."

"No, they weren't." He pulled into the hospital parking lot, coming to a halt in front of the ER doors. "But that doesn't mean I'm a good guy."

"I don't believe that. A person can only go on acting like someone they're not for so long before the facade breaks. You're really *that* person, Kellan. You're that generous, giving guy. It's not your penance, it's not an act. It's you. You aren't like Peanut's dad, and I'm sorry I've let him define my view of you and your actions."

He held her gaze in the rearview mirror, his heart about to explode out of his chest. Then he chided himself for sitting there and not being useful. With the click of the seat belt, he hurried out and tugged the back door open for her. "I'm the one who's sorry, Paige."

"You'll forgive me?" Her hand went to his cheek, cool and soft.

"There's nothing to forgive, Paige. But if Peanut's hurt?"

"I'm wondering what's up with Peanut, myself," Joyce chimed in. "You're talking a lot for someone in serious pain, Paige."

"You're right." Paige's eyes went wide. "Because I'm not in any pain. I haven't had any pangs since Main Street. I didn't even realize. Maybe it wasn't labor, after all."

"Or maybe you're between contractions. I think you'd better get checked out, anyway." Kellan wasn't one to come up with worst-case scenarios, but he couldn't prevent a few scary thoughts from flying across his brain. "I'm getting you a wheelchair."

Thankfully, Paige didn't protest. Her mom helped her out of the truck cab and into the wheelchair Kellan had found just inside the ER doors. A scrub-clad nurse bustled after him and guided the wheelchair out of Kellan's hands. "You'll need to move your car, sir."

"Yeah. Sure."

"I'm going in with Paige," Joyce said.

"Of course."

But before Paige was wheeled through the doors into the ER, she turned her head and met his gaze. Her eyes were fierce, narrowed in warning. "I'm not finished with you, Kellan. So don't go too far, please."

"I won't."

He wasn't finished with her, either. Not by a long shot.

Chapter Eighteen

❧

"Dr. Graves said it wasn't labor. I'm fine," Paige reminded everyone, but no one in her tiny house seemed to be listening. Or at least, they weren't stopping what they were doing to acknowledge her in the recliner.

Paige had spent a few hours in the ER, ruling out infections, preeclampsia or any other dangers to the baby before Dr. Graves decided the pain was Braxton-Hicks contractions. She scheduled a follow-up appointment in two days, just in case.

Kellan drove her and Mom back to the tiny house, where they were met by a small crowd—Marigold, Eileen, Aunt Trudie, and even Belinda and Don, who had tidied up Open Book after the baby shower. Now they all crammed into Paige's tiny house, busy as proverbial bees in a minuscule hive.

Eileen transferred the remainder of her chocolate cake into a smaller Tupperware. Aunt Trudie mixed up a batch of tuna salad for Paige to eat "later." Whenever that was.

Mom stacked the baby gifts with their cards atop the bookshelf. Marigold tied the blue-and-pink balloons to the back of a chair. Belinda made coffee while Don, the only other person seated other than Paige, stared at the balloons. "That knot won't hold, Marigold."

Marigold giggled. "You rhymed, Don. Well done."

His snuffle announced he hadn't intended to rhyme. "You've got to double knot it."

Kellan brought Paige a glass of water. "Doing okay?"

"I'm fabulous, which is why no one should be fussing."

"Let us fuss," he said.

"Well, I have an announcement." Paige cupped her hands around her mouth. "Can everyone hear me?"

"Yes." Everyone glanced at her, but no one stopped what they were doing.

"I'm staying in Widow's Peak Creek."

Mom paused then, her fingers trailing from the edge of the white crocheted baby blanket she'd just folded. "For how long?"

"For—I don't know. Until God tells me otherwise. But I want Peanut to be born here."

"You've established rapport with your doctor. I get it," Mom said. "But it won't be as easy for me to help you from Sacramento."

"I appreciate your desire to help, Mom. Really. But I'm okay. I can make this work myself. Support myself. In God's strength, of course, but if I falter, I have Him. And I have friends who care for me, in a way I've never had friends before." Her gaze met Kellan's, but it was hard to tell what she was thinking. "Widow's Peak Creek is my home now."

Most everyone in the room cheered, but Kellan ran his hand over his mouth, as if contemplating something. Mom rushed to the recliner, hands on the arms, towering over Paige.

"I don't think this is a good idea. You're vulnerable. Needy."

"I may be vulnerable, but I'm not needy. I can take care of myself, Mom, despite you saying otherwise. It's…it's hurtful, you saying that."

"I'm sorry. I never wanted to hurt you. My goal was to keep you safe, you and Drew. But I lost him, anyway." Mom's hands flapped in that way of women who don't know what to say. "I can't control everything, can I?"

"No, we can't." Paige understood her mom's

impulse to try, though. It was human nature. "Maybe we can talk to Benton about that, Mom. Letting God have control."

"Maybe." It was the closest her mom had come to being willing to talk about God, ever.

"You won't lose me. Or Peanut. I want you to be active in his or her life, Mom. If that's what you want."

"Of course it's what I want." Mom didn't cry, but she reached to enfold Paige in her arms and held on a long time.

Everyone else had made themselves busy during the exchange, and if they overheard much, they didn't show it. There was a half-hearted argument going on in the kitchen over tuna salad recipes, with Kellan and his mom chiming in on the debate between sweet pickles and dill pickles.

Kellan was clearly half-listening for Paige to be finished, though, because he caught her eye the moment she and Mom ended their hug. He sidled back into the living room area. "Anything I can do for you, Paige?"

"Actually, I was thinking that you and I could go look at the poppies out front."

"The poppies are faded, Paige dear." Marigold fussed with the balloon strings. "It's been too hot for them."

Paige stood, anyway. "Then I'd like to visit Sydney. I need some fresh air."

"I'll go with you." Don pushed up from the couch.

"Donald Phelps, you sit back down," Belinda whispered through a clenched jaw.

"It's crowded in here," he protested.

"It'll be less crowded when we're outside." Kellan's lips twitched as he gestured for Paige to lead the way. "Come on."

They could hear the group inside the tiny house, hissing whispers as they made their way onto the porch. Paige bit back a smile. She had no idea what to expect, but she had some things to say. Their unfinished discussion while she was being wheeled into the hospital left a lot of things unsaid.

It didn't take long at all to reach the gate to Kellan's backyard. The instant the gate latch clunked open, three woofing dogs dashed from the patio. "Well, hello there." Paige greeted sleek Jet, fluffy Gladys and little Sydney with vigorous pats as they wove around her legs.

"They think you're pretty fabulous." Kellan shut the gate behind them.

"I think they're fabulous, too. And Frank, too, wherever he is."

"Right there on the lounge chair."

Sure enough, the gray cat had made himself comfortable on the chaise, his posture relaxed and his gaze fixed at some point in the distance, but his ears turned toward them like perky, triangular satellite dishes, attesting to the fact that he knew very well they were there.

She rubbed his silky head. "Hi, Frank."

He blinked slowly.

Kellan waited, hands in his pockets. "Want to sit on the swing or the chairs?"

"The swing. Obviously."

"Obviously." Kellan followed her to the white-painted swing, but didn't sit down with her. "Comfortable?"

"Pain free." But *comfortable* wasn't the word she'd choose, not with him standing there, looking unsure what to do. She patted the spot beside her. "Can we go back to being friends?"

"I'd like that. If you're sure."

"I'm sure."

He sat down then, leaving a good several inches between them. "There are a few things I need to say, though, and you might not want to be friends when I'm done."

Panic zipped over her skin. "Such as?"

"Well, I've agreed to open a second bookstore with Don. In Pinehurst."

Why would that bother her? "You were so opposed to it."

"I saw your note today. One you left in the

office when you were working on the book drive data. About a book drive for the veterans' center in Pinehurst?"

"Yeah?" She'd forgotten all about that.

"I was talking to Benton today, and he helped me see I've been holding back on some things because I don't think I deserve them. And the truth is, I can see several benefits in expanding to two stores. In Pinehurst, in particular." He gazed at her out of the corner of his eyes. "The building we're eyeing is located a few doors down from the veterans' center. Your note got me thinking, and well, if I have a store in Pinehurst, I can help different groups, including theirs. And I'm also going to attend their meetings. Talk with other vets about our experiences. And fill up their bookroom, of course."

"Of course." She laughed. "I think those are great ideas, Kellan."

"I want to be healthier. In every way. Be helped and help other people, too, if I can."

Bear one another's burdens.

"I don't want to be in Pinehurst a lot, though." His toe nudged the swing into gentle motion. "My heart is here."

"In Widow's Peak Creek."

"Yes, but I also mean *here*." His gaze met hers, his eyes an intense shade of blue, before dropping his gaze to her hands. Like he wanted to take them. "I don't want to cross any lines. I've come closer to that than I should have—or maybe I did go too far, back in the alley when we found Sydney. Remember? And at the hospital, I kissed your fingers. But I was your boss—"

"I never thought of you as a boss. Not like that, so if this is you being worried about an inequality of power between us, that's out the window, as far as I'm concerned. You might still be my landlord, technically, but you and I were never just those things, boss and employee, landlord and tenant. Or even two people who came together because we both lost Drew. We were connected by more than that from the beginning, if I'm being honest."

"You felt it, too?" His pinkie extended toward hers. The light brush of it was like fire.

She shut her eyes for a moment. "I didn't want to think about what I felt, but yes. From the first time I met you. So please, let's be honest and open. Fully. It's just you and me here. Well, and the dogs." Sydney was hard to ignore, since she was snuffling around Paige's foot like Paige had stuffed a doggy treat in her shoe. "Tell me, Kellan."

He didn't resist when she took his hand. His clasp could mean a million things. All the while Paige's heart pounded against her rib cage like a wild thing. *Lord, give me words to say. And the patience to wait while he says what he needs to get off his chest.*

"I know you said you're not going to be in a relationship, for your sake, but most of all for Peanut's. You were betrayed by Peanut's dad, and I know that I betrayed your trust, too. I respect that. But I've changed my mind about what I want."

"What do you want, Kellan?"

His blue-eyed gaze met hers, sincere, and oh, my goodness. Something else she'd never seen. "I said I wanted to be single, but I don't. I want a family. I want you, Paige. I tried not to, but I fell in love with you."

The sky might be clear, but it felt like a bolt of lightning struck the ground beneath her, making the hair on her arms stand on end. "You love me."

"And Peanut," he added, his eyes softening. "When you went into early labor, and I thought we could lose him? Or her? I couldn't bear it."

"I know." She hadn't fully realized it until now. "You care about the baby, and you've been there for us at every turn."

"If you let me stay in your life, though, I'll respect your boundaries. Peanut comes first for you, and you've chosen to stay single. And if you want to come back to Open Book, I'll be strictly professional. But knowing how I feel, I wanted you to know that if you ever change your mind about me—about the possibility of us—that I have no more secrets. I'll never keep another thing from you. I'll do whatever it takes to be with you, because you are the one I love, Paige. Your smile. Your warmth. You're like sunshine to me. God used our unconventional friendship to show me things about myself. To help me heal. You don't want to be helped, Paige, but you have to know how much you've helped me. And I'll always be grateful."

He lifted their clasped hands and pressed his lips to the back of her fingers. "Kellan Lambert, that was quite a speech. I'm putty right now."

"Really?" His brow arched. A little smug, even. "Well, at least I've given you something to think about for when you're ready."

"I'm ready now."

"Don't you want to take some time?"

"I don't need any. I don't want to waste another second. I wanted to protect Peanut from hurt, but you won't ever hurt him. Or her. You are worthy of trust. I love you, Kellan, and I want to stay in Widow's Peak Creek. I want to help bear your burdens and accept your help with mine. It won't be easy for me, though. I've been in this mode a long time."

"We can help each other work toward a healthier balance." He fully faced her on the swing now, his clasp on her hand tighter than it had been. "You really love me?"

"I do. But I'm not coming back to Open Book."

"Oh?"

"I'm taking a job at the preschool while I finish my courses. I already texted Jane, when I was waiting to get discharged from the ER. It's three hours a day, sharing the job with another aide. Jane is pretty sure there will be a full-time job available by the time Peanut and I are ready for that change."

"Are you serious? That's fabulous. Your dream is coming true, Paige. I'm so happy."

He really was. No one in her life had ever been as excited about her goals as he had been.

"I'm happy, too Especially that you're not my boss anymore. So I can do this." She tugged his hands and drew him closer.

"That's a good reason." He bent his head and oh, the touch of his lips on hers made her head spin.

Too soon, he pulled back and rested his forehead on hers. "I love you, but we're in full view of our relatives."

Her blush burned all the way to her earlobes. "Oh, my."

But she was happy enough settled in the circle of his arms, gently rocking on the porch swing, with the dogs frolicking on the grass and the silhouettes of their loved ones peeking out at them from the windows of the tiny house. She'd never known love like this. But God, and Kellan, had opened her eyes and heart to new possibilities. A richer way of living. One bound to others, helping one another along the journey.

And resting her cheek against Kellan's chest, listening to the firm, steady beat of his heart, she couldn't wait to see what God had in store for them.

Epilogue

Eleven weeks later

Despite having had preterm labor, in the end, Paige delivered a healthy seven-pound baby only one week before her due date, just as the five-lobed leaves of the sweetgum tree outside their house began to turn fiery red.

Once the baby was settled in Paige's arms, Kellan brushed a few strands of dark hair from his wife's cheek and pressed a kiss onto her damp brow. "You did it. I'm so proud of you."

She smiled up at him, her eyes tired but full of love and joy. "I can't stop looking at her."

"I can't stop looking at either one of you. My girls." He kissed the baby's brow, too—or rather, he kissed the knit peach cap snuggled over her head. The sleeping baby snuffled in response. "I am so blessed that God brought our lives together, Paige."

"Come here." Her hand cupped the back of his neck and pulled him down for a brief kiss. They lingered, foreheads touching, baby between them, for the span of a few breaths. "You were an amazing coach. You remembered all the breathing techniques."

"Must be from all of my endurance cycling," he joked.

"You were also amazing, being in here, focusing on me." Her gaze darkened, serious. "Did you struggle at all, being in a hospital?"

Weary as she was, she was worried about him being triggered. "None." The birthing center didn't look much like a hospital, which helped, but once or twice something had caused his pulse to spike. Rather than fight it, he'd noted his response and spoken briefly to God about it, employing some of the relaxation techniques suggested by fellow members of his veterans' group in Pinehurst. Including Herb, whom he'd invited. Herb was so active there now with his new friends, he only dropped in Open Book for the coffee twice a week, but there was always fresh coffee on hand for him if he came by.

But aside from what he'd learned from his peers, Kellan was also keenly aware that his memories were being healed by God. As Benton had said, once they'd been exposed to the light and he'd been able to openly grapple with the past, he'd received God's forgiveness and forgiven himself. And he'd been able to ask Paige to marry him with no secrets between them.

Their courtship had been short, true, but they could trust each other. Neither of them was going anywhere. And they didn't want to wait. They wanted to be a family.

"I love you both." He'd said it before, but he would never get tired of repeating it.

"I love you, too. Want to hold her, Daddy?"

More than anything. She was safely ensconced in his arms—so tiny, light as air, almost—and he and Paige marveled in the masterpiece of her, from her ears to her nose and rosebud lips. *Thank you for making me her father, Lord. I don't deserve this.*

A soft knock rapped against the door. "May we come in?" The familiar high voice sounded excited.

"Of course, Marigold. Oh, Auntie! Eileen, come in." Paige's voice was as cheerful as Marigold's.

The three women tiptoed inside, laden with gifts, balloons and a vase of flowers. "Iceland poppies," Paige marveled. "Marigold, where did you get those in autumn?"

"I've been sneaky, growing them in my spare bedroom, praying there'd be a few blooming for this special occasion. And there'll be some growing in the flower bed at your house when you get back, too, and the tiny house, but I don't expect those to bloom for a week or two yet."

"I'm looking forward to it. As well as getting Peanut home." Paige grinned as Kellan handed the baby to Aunt Trudie, who'd just scrubbed up at the sink.

"Surely Peanut has a real name now." Trudie glanced up from the baby.

"Poppy Elizabeth," Paige announced. For her favorite flower. For the beauty and grace and brightness of its blooms. For the way it grew tall and beautiful in difficult soil, spreading cheer despite its circumstances. Grace and joy and endurance—traits she and Kellan hoped for their daughter.

The baby was passed among the trio of matchmakers, and within minutes the room crowded with new arrivals. Paige's mom, pink-cheeked with excitement, followed by Pastor Benton, who'd directed her to a church near her house where she had become a regular attendee. Kellan's mom and stepdad arrived next, and though they hadn't made the choice to follow Jesus, Kellan and Paige still prayed for them.

Paige tugged Kellan's hand, softly drawing his attention. "I thought it would be me and the baby alone, forever. But you are the husband and father I always hoped for. And now I have all of this." Her gaze scanned the room. "A large, loving family."

Even though he was related to a good number of the people in this room, he'd never felt free to embrace the life of a family—not just committing himself to a wife and child, but the others in the room he'd known and cared for but whom he hadn't allowed to know him for who he really was.

He planted another soft kiss on her brow. "I may have known them all for years, but because of you—and God—I have them, too. In a rich, wonderful way I never expected."

"Me? I didn't do anything but visit Widow's Peak Creek."

"You stayed."

"Well, I couldn't leave Sydney. She's too cute," she teased. "And Gladys and Jet need me, too. Frank doesn't need me, per se, but he does like cuddling up on the couch."

"He does. And your preschool kids adore you."

"It's mutual." Her work as an aide at Little Lambs would soon lead to a teacher position, but Paige was grateful for the flexibility her aide position allowed her as the mom of a newborn.

"She's a pretty thing," Don said, although he held Poppy at a distance, like she was a ticking time bomb.

Sure enough, Poppy let out a sharp, piercing cry, and Don hastily rushed the bundled infant to Kellan. His daughter's tiny face was wrinkled, red and decidedly displeased.

"That's our cue to go," Aunt Trudie announced.

"See you later, dears?" Marigold confirmed.

"I'll drop off my chocolate cake tomorrow," Gran said.

Benton, Don and Belinda likewise bid them farewell for now, but Joyce took one last, longing look at baby Poppy. "I'll see you tomorrow at home."

She'd always told herself there was blue sky behind the dark clouds. And here it was, her blue sky.

A home with Kellan and their daughter. A place of rest and hope. And love. So much love.

* * * * *

If you enjoyed this story, look for
A Future for His Twins
by Susanne Dietze.

Dear Reader,

Thank you for visiting Widow's Peak Creek! While plotting the first book of the series, *A Future for His Twins*, Kellan appeared in my brain with a cat named Frank and a smile that I knew covered over some serious pain. Who was this guy? I had to find out.

Each person we meet bears some sort of burden. Kellan and Paige find it easier to help others than to accept help, but they learn God often uses our relationships with others—including sharing one another's burdens—to work out His plan.

This story was written while I was isolated with my family due to COVID-19. My prayers continue for everyone affected by the virus: the sick, essential workers, those who mourn and those who struggle in any other way. May the Lord bless you.

I'd be remiss if I didn't thank God for His help and provision, my family and friends, my agent, Tamela, my editor, Emily, the Love Inspired team and you, readers, for allowing me this opportunity.

Special thanks are due to Jennifer Coburn, my favorite preschool director in the universe, who answered all of my questions and whose programs helped inspire those in the book. As always, any mistakes in this book are mine alone.

If you're online, I'd love to connect! My website is www.SusanneDietze.com, and if you visit, you can sign up for my short but sweet newsletters for freebies, recipes and other fun stuff. I'm also on Facebook at SusanneDietzeBooks, and Instagram and Twitter as SusanneDietze.

Blessings,
Susanne

Get 4 FREE REWARDS!

We'll send you 2 FREE Books plus 2 FREE Mystery Gifts.

Love Inspired Suspense books showcase how courage and optimism unite in stories of faith and love in the face of danger.

FREE Value Over $20

YES! Please send me 2 FREE Love Inspired Suspense novels and my 2 FREE mystery gifts (gifts are worth about $10 retail). After receiving them, if I don't wish to receive any more books, I can return the shipping statement marked "cancel." If I don't cancel, I will receive 6 brand-new novels every month and be billed just $5.24 each for the regular-print edition or $5.99 each for the larger-print edition in the U.S., or $5.74 each for the regular-print edition or $6.24 each for the larger-print edition in Canada. That's a savings of at least 13% off the cover price. It's quite a bargain! Shipping and handling is just 50¢ per book in the U.S. and $1.25 per book in Canada.* I understand that accepting the 2 free books and gifts places me under no obligation to buy anything. I can always return a shipment and cancel at any time. The free books and gifts are mine to keep no matter what I decide.

Choose one: ☐ **Love Inspired Suspense Regular-Print** (153/353 IDN GNWN) ☐ **Love Inspired Suspense Larger-Print** (107/307 IDN GNWN)

Name (please print)

Address   Apt. #

City   State/Province   Zip/Postal Code

Email: Please check this box ☐ if you would like to receive newsletters and promotional emails from Harlequin Enterprises ULC and its affiliates. You can unsubscribe anytime.

Mail to the Harlequin Reader Service:
IN U.S.A.: P.O. Box 1341, Buffalo, NY 14240-8531
IN CANADA: P.O. Box 603, Fort Erie, Ontario L2A 5X3

Want to try 2 free books from another series? Call 1-800-873-8635 or visit www.ReaderService.com.

LIS21R

Get 4 FREE REWARDS!

We'll send you 2 FREE Books <u>plus</u> 2 FREE Mystery Gifts.

Harlequin Heartwarming Larger-Print books will connect you to uplifting stories where the bonds of friendship, family and community unite.

FREE Value Over **$20**